Cover Copy

Traveling through time…for a Highlander.

Wearing the four-hundred-year-old amulet she inherited, Marie MacLean enters a faerie circle near the ruins of Dunyvaig Castle. A veil rises. A warrior from the past makes a wish to win the war against the Chief of MacLean, and as the veil thins, she falls through into his time.

Highland warrior Archie MacDonald has been gifted a faerie who insists she's from the future and the progeny of both his and his enemy's clan. The last thing he expects is for her to stir him on a level he's never experienced before. All he needs is her aid in the war, no matter where she believes she's from.

Determined to keep history on course, Marie enters the crux of the battle. She must ensure the MacLean chief who has yet to father her paternal line isn't killed, and all without perishing herself. Can Archie see past his need for revenge before he kills his enemy? If he wishes to save the woman who's crossed centuries to be by his side, he must.

Books by Joanne Wadsworth

The Matheson Brothers Series
Highlander's Desire, Book One
Highlander's Passion, Book Two
Highlander's Seduction, Book Three
Highlander's Kiss, Book Four
Highlander's Heart, Book Five
Highlander's Sword, Book Six
Highlander's Bride, Book Seven
Highlander's Caress, Book Eight
Highlander's Touch, Book Nine
Highlander's Shifter, Book Ten
Highlander's Claim, Book Eleven
Highlander's Courage, Book Twelve
Highlander's Mermaid, Book Thirteen

Highlander Heat Series
Highlander's Castle, Book One
Highlander's Magic, Book Two
Highlander's Charm, Book Three
Highlander's Guardian, Book Four
Highlander's Faerie, Book Five
Highlander's Champion, Book Six
Highlander's Captive (Short Story)

Billionaire Bodyguards Series
Billionaire Bodyguard Attraction, Book One
Billionaire Bodyguard Boss, Book Two
Billionaire Bodyguard Fling, Book Three

Books by Joanne Wadsworth

Regency Brides Series
The Duke's Bride, Book One
The Earl's Bride, Book Two
The Wartime Bride, Book Three
The Earl's Secret Bride, Book Four
The Prince's Bride, Book Five
Her Pirate Prince, Book Six

Princesses of Myth Series
Protector, Book One
Warrior, Book Two
Hunter (Short Story - Included in Warrior, Book Two)
Enchanter, Book Three
Healer, Book Four
Chaser, Book Five

Highlander's Magic

Highlander Heat, Book Two

JOANNE WADSWORTH

Highlander's Magic
ISBN-13: 978-1-99-003423-7
Copyright © 2014, Joanne Wadsworth
Edited by Penny Barber
Cover Art by Joanne Wadsworth
First electronic publication: June 2014

Joanne Wadsworth
http://www.joannewadsworth.com

AUTHOR'S NOTE:
This book is a work of fiction. The names, characters, places, and incidents are products of the writer's imagination or have been used fictitiously and are not to be construed as real. Any resemblance to persons, living or dead, actual events, locale or organizations is entirely coincidental. The author does not have any control over and does not assume any responsibility for third-party websites or their content.

Published in the United States of America

First digital publication: June 2014
First print publication: September 2014

Dedication

For my son, Rocco, who adores animals and has such a caring heart. Hugs.

Acknowledgements

Huge thanks go to my hubby, Jason, and kiddies, Marisa, Caleb, Cruise and Rocco, an incredibly supportive family who allow me so much time to write. My love for you is endless.

I also have the most amazing editor, Penny Barber. The absolute best.

For my readers, I can't thank you enough for joining me, and taking this journey to where imagination and magic soar.

Chapter 1

The ruins of Dunyvaig Castle, on the Isle of Islay, Scotland.

"I can't believe these ruins were once the home of Mum's MacDonald ancestors." Marie MacLean belted her white woolen coat tighter. Dunyvaig Castle had stood guard over this sought after entrance of Lagavulin Bay, when a powerful stronghold and sea base meant the difference between life and death.

"Clan MacDonald ruled Islay centuries ago." Katherine, her twin, flapped her tour brochure open where they stood high on the craggy rise. "Yet Dad's clan MacLean ancestors continually feuded with them from the nearby isles. We're like the progeny of two bickering clans who knew very little peace."

"What about poor Mary?" Marie rubbed the silver amulet at her neck. The MacDonald clan crest was engraved on one side, and on the reverse, the MacLean's crest. "The two clans should have come together in harmony the day Mary MacLean wed the MacDonald chief. Instead the feud became bitterer."

"Does the feud intrigue you because of Mary's gift?"

"Absolutely. Mary bequeathed this amulet to her eldest daughter requesting it be passed down through the generations until it once again came into the possession of a MacLean. That took over four-hundred years. It's as if Mary is trying to send me a message, only I've no idea what."

"And you're definitely the eldest daughter of both a MacDonald and a MacLean, Marie. She wanted you to have her amulet."

"Yes, but what am I supposed to do with it?" She hadn't removed Mary's gift since receiving it a few months ago on her twenty-first birthday. Mere weeks before Mum lost her battle with cancer, she'd placed it around her neck. Mum's final wish had been for her and Katherine to bring the amulet home to Dunyvaig Castle as Mary had requested. So halfway around the world they'd traveled, from Australia's Gold Coast, and then by ferry from Scotland's mainland to this isle.

Such a rugged, yet beautiful land. Marie lifted her face toward the sky. It would be even more picturesque if the heavy gray clouds above diffused. "It looks like we're in for some bad weather."

"A storm I'd say. It's strange how their seasons are in the reverse to ours. It's autumn here, while Down Under we left spring behind. Everything feels off kilter." Katherine ambled into Dunyvaig's faerie circle and sat on the center stone. The tartan red and blue of her woolen coat made her a bright beacon of color. "Come and sit with me."

Marie perched on the edge of the large flat stone. "Why are we sitting when we should be exploring?"

"Because I'm going to help you figure out what to do with Mary's amulet."

"I wish Mary had left more precise instructions."

"Well, Mum said we had to—" Katherine blinked furiously, suddenly fighting tears.

They talked about Mum all the time, but grief still consumed them. She'd been forty-five. In the prime of her life.

Katherine scrubbed a hand over her face, composing herself. "I'm sorry. I miss Mum so much. This would've been the trip of a lifetime for her."

"Which is why we promised her we'd come. We're going to live her dreams for her. At least we get to do this together." She hugged Katherine, and her sister's sweet vanilla scent, the same as what their mother had worn, soothed her. It wasn't fair they'd lost both their parents. Dad a year past, and now Mum. It was only her and Katherine.

"Promise me you'll never leave me like they did." Katherine squeezed her back.

"I promise. I love you." Her sister was her life.

"I love you too." Katherine let out a long breath. "So, back to the amulet. You brought it here to Dunyvaig. We can check off that request."

"The first and only request following the bestowment. Hmm, maybe if we look around I might have an epiphany." This place was so remote with its grassy moors rolling for miles in both directions.

"Good idea. Let's do that. This faerie circle is pretty amazing. Let me take a picture of us before we leave it." Katherine lugged her cell phone from her jeans pocket and readied it for a shot. "Get closer, sis."

She flattened her cheek to Katherine's and smiled. Throughout their lives, they'd done everything together, and this was yet another adventure.

"Smile." Katherine clicked and checked the picture. "Mirror images. I could've just taken a photo of me and not worried about you."

"You say that all the time." She knocked her shoulder against Katherine's, rose and wandered inside the circle. "I wonder how the faeries got these stones here. They're massive." Nine six-foot high stones stood six feet apart around the perimeter. A tenth stone, short enough to sit on but still as wide, sat plumb in the center. "What else does the brochure say about this circle, other than it's sacred?"

"Just to watch for changes within. It can go from still to wildly windy, but most of all, if a haze surrounds it, the faeries are at play."

"A haze? You mean like—"

Thunder rumbled out at sea, and birds nesting along the rocky shoreline cackled and took flight. Their wings brushed the water as they flew across the inlet to the rushes hugging the other side's marshy edge.

"Bad weather is getting closer, Marie. Maybe we should come back and explore tomorrow." Her sister stood.

"We can give it more time. If need be, we'll make a mad dash to the car. This is a magical circle. Perhaps we could simply wish for fine weather."

"Wishes shouldn't be squandered on weather." A gleam lit Katherine's eyes. "If we're going to make one, it has to be interesting."

Katherine had always loved to make wishes, by the first star she saw at night, to blowing out her birthday candles, to when she lost an eyelash. She'd never been able to stop her sister from making them.

"Come on." Katherine gripped her hands. "I'll make a wish for something both of us have always wanted."

"I'd like an endless supply of chocolate." That would be fabulous.

Katherine chuckled. "Yeah, we can buy chocolate anytime. How about an endless supply of adventure? You can't always buy that."

"Sure. It's why we're here."

"Great." Katherine winked. "Then here's my wish. To the faerie folk of Dunyvaig Castle, I wish for a moment of magic, for Marie and me to live, for us to have untold adventure on your stunning isle. Bring on the fun. Bring on the—"

Thunder boomed and lightning slashed the rippling waves of the bay with a sizzling crackle.

"Okay, I think a mad dash is now in order." She lugged Katherine toward the edge of the circle, hit a hazy barrier and bounced to the ground. "Ouch." She rubbed her nose. "Where'd that come from?"

"Whoa." Gaping, Katherine hauled her to her feet. "It's like a veil's come down."

"You mean you weren't joking when you mentioned the haze?" Beyond the fog, the darkening waves rolled in with a pounding crash.

"This can't be right." Katherine inched forward and patted the sides. "Except there's really something here. How do we get out?"

"Try the other side." This place already spoke of mystery and intrigue, and now it had ramped right up.

"I thought the brochure was simply playing up the whole mystical fae thing." Katherine tapped around the perimeter, knocking on something solid, yet nothing but foggy air swirled. She shot her a wide-eyed look. "Obviously not, and I just made a wish."

"There's got to be a way out. Even if we have to dig, we'll find it." Marie grabbed her sister's hand. Low cloud lit with lightning coasted across the sea. Within the mist a vessel materialized, one reminiscent of a sixteenth century Highland birlinn. "Do you see that, sis? Or is my imagination really going wild?"

Katherine gasped. "A-are those warriors onboard that thing?"

Thirty or so armed men wearing green and blue plaids plunged their oars into the sea and powered their vessel in. At the helm, a commanding man pumped his fist into the air and bellowed orders for his men to lower the sail.

"I…um…I'd say so."

"They're heading right toward us." Katherine pressed her palms against the barrier. "I think my wish just got a whole lot more adventurous than I expected."

"Y-yeah, you're banned now from making—look at the ruins." The manned birlinn now appeared to be the least of her and Katherine's problems. "You see the castle, right?"

Her sister gawked past the clingy mist. "Holy moly. Birlinns. Warriors. Do you think we just fell back through time?"

"Either that or the locals play out reenactments, of an incredibly spectacular sort." She scrubbed her eyes with her knuckles, but the castle remained, standing three stories high on the hill. Battlements topped fortified walls, and candles lit tower windows. In the descending dark, the castle guarded the bay like a sentinel.

"'Tis our captain, Archie MacDonald," a guardsmen called as he rushed along the top of the barbican. This was too real to be a reenactment. No one could rebuild a castle in seconds.

A portcullis rose from within the stone-arched entrance gate, its clunky chains reverberating across the moors. Boots clipped loudly on the stones as a warrior strode out in leather pants and a thick fur vest over a dark linen shirt. He halted at the edge of their circle. "Prepare the great hall for our men's arrival." He palmed the hilt of the sword at his side. "My brother returns."

Marie waved her hand in front of the warrior. "Okay, he can't see us but we can see him. We must be between times, protected somehow by the veil."

"Here, but not here." Katherine glanced at the bay. "Those men are huge. Look at the size of them."

Talk about intimidating. Highlanders, and clearly born of Vikings. Onboard, the men slashed their oars in the reverse direction and slowed their vessel. It skimmed the water as it cruised to the sea-gate. With another booming command from the captain, two of the men leaped into the waist-deep water, seized the bow and roped it to a catch alongside the stone landing.

One by one, they disembarked, jogged up the trail and disappeared into the keep. The captain followed, veering toward the warrior standing before them. "John, is all well?"

"Well enough. Welcome home, Archie." John grasped the captain's shoulders. "Do you have any further word on the chief?"

"I have but 'tis no' good. The king's men have apprehended Angus, as well as his brother, Donald MacDonald of Sleat. I spoke with Donald's second at Dunscaith Castle afore I traveled to Edinburgh."

"You've been all the way to see the king?"

"Aye. Angus is being kept under strict guard, in the highest level of the tower. He and Donald have their own chambers. They're together, yet isolated from the other prisoners." He paced, displaying a massive two-handed claymore holstered to his broad back.

A warrior born to fight, wearing a great plaid secured over his chest with a silver pin and belted low at his waist with a leather girdle. She surely wouldn't mind meeting a man like— oh, what was she thinking? Admiring a man when she and Katherine were trapped like this. Where was her head?

Archie stopped, planted his feet wide. "There isnae any way to rescue him, or at least no' since our arrival raised suspicion and the number of guards increased. I left after being permitted a short conversation with him."

"What did he say? Why was he taken?"

"Angus spoke of a missive he received from the king requesting he present himself at court to atone for his feuding with Mary's brother, the MacLean of Duart. The missive had gone to all three chiefs involved in the feud, including Donald. Angus had no intention of presenting himself, but seeking further counsel with his brother when he made the trip to Skye. The king's men caught him. Donald as well."

"Hell, the king needs to leave us alone to resolve our own

issues, no' alter the way we settle our disputes. He clearly wishes to stamp his mark of ownership on the isles, to control us as he does the rest of Scotland." John clenched his fists. "Angus should have taken more care. Mary is so close to giving birth."

"There's naught we can do about Angus, no' since the king will have his way. Angus said the king is after a settlement, but without Lachlan MacLean, naught can be conferred. I say 'tis better MacLean be removed from the discussions. Angus believes so too. He instructed me to see to MacLean's death, ensuring the king no longer has a reason to hold either him or his brother."

Marie grabbed Katherine. "He must be talking about Mary after she wed Angus MacDonald. We must have arrived at some point in the late 1500s."

"That'd make sense since you're wearing Mary's amulet from that time and this circle brought us here. Do you recall anything about the king capturing Angus and Donald MacDonald because of the feud? I didn't read up like you did before we came."

"I do. All three chiefs involved were taken, but I'm not sure how long they were held. Mary must be here somewhere." Incredibly, history was unfolding before her eyes. "Archie certainly can't kill MacLean as he's said though. If he did, he'd alter history. The king wished an intervention, and all three chiefs entered the discussion." Damn, she couldn't recall if the talks had helped though.

"We're in a different time, sis. History has yet to occur. Maybe we've been brought here for a reason. This has to have something to do with your—"

"There's a haze over the circle this eve." Archie rubbed the towering stone nearest Marie. "Mayhap a touch of faerie magic wouldnae go amiss in winning this war against MacLean. He has to die."

John stepped in beside Archie. "It does appear the faerie

folk are at play."

Mischievous imps for sure. These two warriors didn't know the half of it.

Archie pressed his palm against the veil. His shoulder-length brown hair wisped with blond fluttered in the night breeze. Marie edged closer to him. Gorgeous, if a warrior could be called such. His chin, sharply defined with a deep cleft in the center, held rugged appeal, and his eyes were a stunning shade of molten gold. She might drown in those liquid depths. "Archie, don't make that wish and change history," she murmured. "MacLean can't die. It's not his time."

"Did you hear that?" Archie frowned, shaking his head. "I swear I heard something. Whispers from within. Mayhap the faerie folk wish to aid us. We certainly cannae become vulnerable to an attack should MacLean take this opportunity to stake his revenge. Word will soon spread of Angus and Donald's capture, if it has no' already."

"No. I said MacLean can't die. Don't do it." She pressed her hand against the barrier an inch from the warrior's hand. Electricity buzzed through her, raising the hairs on her arms in a delicious, tingly way. She tried to inch closer.

Katherine eyed John across from her and pressed against the veil nearest him. "Maybe this is why Mary wished for the amulet to return home. Maybe she needed help and asked the fae for aid."

"Do you really think so?" If her sister was right, untold adventure was on its way.

"Why else are we here? Fae magic brought us back through time. This isn't a reenactment."

"I know, but what should we do?" Marie edged closer to Archie.

"The whispers grow stronger, brother. Magic hums in the air." Archie's gaze narrowed on her as he searched within.

"Aye, make your wish while I find Mary. I dinnae want her

hearing of Angus's capture afore I can speak to her. The men will be hard-pressed to delay her questioning."

"Go. I'll be with you shortly."

John strode off into the dark.

"Aye, the air vibrates far too strongly no' to state my desire." Archie rubbed the veil. "Guardians of Dunyvaig, I ask for a wish. I seek my chief's return and require your aid in this journey. Send me a sign. I must win this war against MacLean."

The veil shimmered and Marie's pulse spiked. "I can almost touch him, sis. The haze is thinning."

"Marie, I think you should step back," her sister warned.

"Marie?" Archie whispered her name. "The faeries have given me a name."

"He heard you, Katherine." Marie pushed toward him. "I have to warn him not to kill MacLean."

"Come to me, Marie. Mayhap you are the sign." His husky words swarmed her senses as he swept his hand through the air.

Her amulet rose, breached the barrier between them and spun into his palm. She'd tell him in person.

"Wait!" Katherine yanked her coat. "You're not going anywhere without me."

"Hold onto me. He needs us." Wind tunneled around her, whipping her hair across her face.

"Come, my faerie." Archie jerked her amulet.

"Whoa." She lurched through the barrier and slammed into the warrior. His body was solid, his flesh warm and his hold tight.

"Unbelievable." His gaze searched hers. "A faerie in truth. My sign, as I wished."

"I—I—"

The circle was again thick with the haze. But where was Katherine? She should have come with her. She pounded the veil. "Hey, I said to hold on, sis. I don't want to do this on my own. Get here now, or you're going to be in a ton of trouble."

* * * *

Afraid the faerie would get away, Archie gripped her arm as she called out for another. She had a strange accent, like the Lowlanders. "Who is Katherine?"

"My sister. She was right there with me in the circle."

"There is none here but you and me." The faerie's white-blond hair shimmered to her waist, and her eyes shone the deepest shade of midnight-blue. He stroked the soft folds of her white woolen coat. Never had he known such a fine weave. Her legs were covered in white linen, clothing similar to men's trews yet completely feminine. White knee-high leather boots encased her feet. Head to toe, a vision.

'Twas a powerful circle to deliver one holding such magic. The power radiating from this circle had beckoned him time and again over the years. The faeries often played, throwing up a haze or causing the wind to sweep through or become completely still. Now it had brought him her. "Mayhap your sister will come another time?"

"She has to come now. Her wish was for both of us." She struggled to push back in. "I can't leave her behind."

"The veil is strong. I've never been able to pass through when it's risen." He shoved his upper arm against it. "When the haze is gone, you can enter, though none do. 'Tis a sacred place, and now with my wish, the fae have delivered you. Your sister must no' be needed."

"Of course she's needed, and I didn't mean to answer your wish without my sister."

"What does your sister look like?"

"We're identical twins." She grasped his shirt. "I really can't leave her behind. I've got to get back in."

"You dinnae appear to have a choice, otherwise she would have come, or you would have been able to return." Aye, she was here to stay, this faerie with her tiny nose and high cheeks sprinkled with freckles. So young and enchanting. Never had a faerie graced one of his clan with their presence like this. They tinkered and played, but they also guarded their lands, having ensured Dunyvaig never fell into MacLean's hands. "Magic has brought you to me when we need it the most. I have a war to win, and you're a wonder bestowed by the circle. You even wear Mary's amulet. How did you come by it?"

She gripped the piece. "I'm no faerie, just a regular person, and Mary gifted this to me. She left instructions asking I return it to Islay."

"Good. Then you have done as she asked." He cupped her cheek. "Fae you are, your presence one of magic." 'Twas abundantly clear, and she would never convince him otherwise.

"I'm not from this time or place."

"Aye, you've come from your own time and place. The fae live—"

"I didn't mean it that way. I'm really not one of the fae." She glared at the veil then slammed her hands against it. "This is impossible. Guardians of Dunyvaig, I wish to be reunited with Katherine. Send her through, or let me back in. Please, do something."

"Nay, lass. You must stay. See to my wish and then you may go. The guardians willnae keep you here beyond the time you've been sent. I'm certain of it."

"How long will this barrier be up for?"

"It comes and goes, depending on your people."

"The fae aren't my people."

"Aid me, and I promise you my protection." It appeared his faerie didn't wish to accept her destiny. He would convince her otherwise. "No harm shall ever come to you. My word is true."

"My sister and I never do anything without each other."

"Mayhap this is the one time you shall."

"Excuse me, but I'd rather not." Arms crossed, she thumped her foot. "You really don't listen very well."

A woman with fire. Even better. She would need to be

strong in order to grant him his wish. He had a battle ahead of him against MacLean, and the Chief of Duart was no easy adversary. "What would your sister wish you to do right now?"

"Return to her." She huffed then slid Mary's talisman over her head. "Or return to her the moment I'd seen to your wish. Katherine is the adventurous sort. She's probably peeved she's not here right now, as well as freaking out about being alone. I've got to get back to her, and since this talisman brought me here, hopefully it will do the same and bring my sister to me."

"Your words are strange. 'Tis clear you speak of another world."

"No, this world, just a different time." She stepped back then frowned. "Hold on. The veil's lifting."

"Then be quick about what you need to do to bring your sister through. Throw her the amulet afore the veil disperses."

She tossed the talisman and it landed with a clunk on the center stone. "Take the amulet, Katherine. Mary may have bequeathed it to me, but use it to get out as I did." She fanned her hand through the veil as it continued to thin. "Please, hurry."

It shimmered and vanished on the wind, gone as quick as it came. "Lass, the fae are nay more, but they always return. You must now wait."

"No, this can't be happening. I need my sister." She staggered inside and fell to her knees before the center stone. "Katherine, come back."

His heart heaved for her loss, but it wouldn't be for long. "You've come for a reason, Marie. To aid me." He held out his hand. "Come. I shall look after you as I promised."

"I didn't want to do this alone."

"Once you've fulfilled my wish, you can return. I didnae ask for any more than your aid. Come."

She swiped her tears then rose and wobbled toward him. "If I help you, it's because I want to get back to Katherine."

"Aye, lass." A few more steps and she cleared the circle. He caught her around the waist and held her close. His faerie would aid him, just as he needed her to. "Together we cannae fail against MacLean. You'll soon be back with your sister."

"Since I don't have any other choice, tell me where to start. The sooner I'm done here, the sooner I can return."

"'Tis late and I've traveled far this day. We'll begin on the morrow. For now, you're welcome to use my chamber to rest. It overlooks this circle, which should bring you comfort."

"Are you taking me inside?" Her beautiful eyes widened as she glanced at the castle.

"You've naught to fear." Eager to get her within the safety of the Dunyvaig's walls, he tugged her under the arched entrance. "No one would ever harm one of the fae."

Within the inner courtyard, stone buildings rose all around them. He steered Marie up the side stairs, bypassing the great hall where his clan had gathered for the evening meal. Inside his chamber on the third floor, he ushered her in and shut the door.

She hurried to the window, shoved open the wooden shutters and peered through the dark. "I can see the circle, just." She slumped against the stone sill. "I can't believe I've left Katherine behind. It all happened so fast."

"Believe it, lass." He crossed to the fireplace, lit and stoked it into life. It blazed and spread its heat through the room. After taking a candle and lighting it from the flames, he set in in the corner stand next to his bed. The warmth and light should soothe her.

"Please, tell me more about the circle." Her gaze remained glued to it.

"There is never an assurance of when the veil rises, only that it does." He eased in behind her. The stones, lit by the moonlight, appeared ghostly white, and Mary's talisman sparkled atop the center stone. "As no one enters the circle, the amulet will remain within should your sister have need of it."

"Yes, I don't want anyone moving it." She peered at him.

"And it used to be Mary's talisman. I know you don't believe me, but I've told you the truth. She gifted it to me on my twenty-first birthday."

"'Tis impossible."

"I've no reason to lie." She shook her head. "I'll convince you somehow. First, tell me more about the warrior with you before. John. You called him your brother. Could he keep a watch out for my sister? The more who do, the better."

"John is my twin. We are similar but no' identical, and aye, I will have him and the guards keep an eye out. As soon as you're comfortable, I'll go speak with him." If reassurance was what she needed, he could easily provide it.

* * * *

"Yes, speak to him, please. That's what I want." Marie clutched Archie's arm. She would have to see to his wish, which had better not take long. Katherine needed her, would be so worried.

"First, tell me more about your sister." He stroked her back, his touch sending a delicious tingle to her toes. "You said her wish was for both of you. What was it she asked for?"

"For a moment of magic. She wished for us to live and to have untold adventure along the way, although I doubt she meant quite this much adventure." Never this much.

"Will anyone other than her miss your presence?"

"No. Our mother, Marianne MacDonald, passed away a few months ago. Our father, Locky MacLean, the year before." He thought her fae and she had to set him right. Convincing him she was from the twenty-first century wouldn't be an easy task, but she had to try. "I don't want there to be anything but the truth between us. I'm from a time far in the future, and I'm a direct descendent of Mary's, well Mary and Angus's on my mother's side. The amulet I wore was Mary's. I received the family heirloom in my time, through my maternal line. Mary left instructions it be handed from her eldest daughter to her eldest daughter until it once again came into the possession of a daughter born to a MacLean. That's me."

"Angus and Mary's bairns are too young. What you speak of isnae possible."

"You have to keep an open mind. I truly am both MacDonald and MacLean. My name is Marie MacLean. I've traveled here from the year two-thousand and fourteen." She couldn't state it more clearly.

"Nay, lass. There's no need to ply your tricks. Fae you are, and fae you remain." Clicking his tongue as if in admonishment, he strode to the door. "I'll ask a servant to bring a tray. Make yourself comfortable while I speak with John."

"I'm really not fae." She raced after him, snatched his arm. "You have to believe me."

He tweaked her chin. "'Tis the year fifteen-hundred and ninety. Now, no more. On the morrow, you'll work your magic. MacLean must be halted." He closed the paneled door with a thunk. Gone.

Hopefully it didn't matter if he believed her or not, but she'd rather he did. His disbelief didn't change the fact she was now in Scotland though, somewhere far in the past and needed to fulfill his wish before she could return to Katherine.

She stalked to the window, needing to be closer to Katherine even though currently impossible. She'd tried to learn all she could about Mary MacDonald before she'd traveled here, but with over four-hundred years passing, the information had been sparse. More was recorded on her husband, Angus MacDonald, and brother, Lachlan MacLean, both chiefs of their own clans. Although, she'd never quite understood how the intense feud had begun.

Right now, she'd try to seek the answers she needed, and from Mary no less. The task before her was immense. Aid Archie in winning the war, while ensuring he didn't change history and kill MacLean.

Her sister's wish would certainly provide a ton of adventure, and with her own Highland warrior on the side.

But she'd do whatever it took to ensure she returned.

There was no other option.

Katherine needed her, and she needed Katherine.

Chapter 2

Next to John atop the battlements, Archie inspected the faerie circle. Under the moonlight, ten pale stones beckoned with their otherworldly secrets. Marie was his faerie, not Mary's direct descendent. As much as he believed in magic, her traveling from the future was beyond the realm of possibility.

Nay. Mayhap she was concerned about the task set before her, but he'd allay those fears when he rejoined her. He only sought her magic, not for her to undertake the battle against MacLean herself. He'd make it clear.

Had Angus remained at Dunyvaig Castle instead of traveling to Skye to visit his brother, he would never have been captured. And if the king's men had come to Islay, they would have fought to ensure he remained here.

John cleared his throat. "You said Marie fell out of the circle right after you made your wish. 'Tis a miracle, a sure sign we will overcome MacLean."

His twin, so close to him in looks that the odd man mistook them, knew him as no other did. At eight and twenty, his brother was his second, as he himself was Angus's. Together he and John would ensure Islay never fell to MacLean while Angus remained imprisoned. Stroking the dirk hilt strapped at his wrist, he said, "I've offered her my protection and in doing so, yours too."

"Aye, without question she has mine." John scanned the horizon toward neighboring Jura. MacLean held a firm hold on the northern end of the island, but the southern portion was theirs. "Should we expect her sister? Will there soon be two fae in our midst?"

"The veil lifted and the haze cleared. Marie is here. She is the only one the guardians delivered to us. I dinnae believe Katherine will come."

"Does she have any other family apart from her sister?"

"She told me her parents have passed, although she speaks of coming from the future, of being born from Mary's maternal line, her mother a MacDonald and her father a MacLean."

"'Tis impossible." John scoffed.

"As I told her, but she worries for her twin. I'm sure that is the only reason behind her ramblings."

'Twas normal for the eldest to worry. John was a minute younger than he was. Over the years, many had told them twins were nature's gift, although in the days following their birth, Mother had bled to death. No gift at all. They did their best though, fighting for their clan as Father had done. He'd died with honor on the battlefield, albeit under a MacLean's blade.

"Word of Angus's imprisonment will soon spread through the isles. Lachlan MacLean willnae hesitate to use our chief's capture to his advantage." John crossed his arms.

"Then we'll be here to ensure he does no' make any gains. We fight, as we always have. Per mare per terras, by sea and by land."

"Aye." John scrutinized the circle. "Fortune shines upon us. The guardians have sent us a boon, one we—"

A horn trumpeted with one long and eerie blast from the north.

"Damn." John gritted his teeth. "Will guards the coast

toward Jura as you instructed on your leaving. He has no' sounded the horn since our rival's last disturbance."

"It'll be MacLean. Like a rat, he continually returns. I'll rouse the men."

"What of your faerie, Archie?"

"She remains here until I send word all is clear. Secure the keep and maintain a tight guard. Lachlan MacLean is devious, but I'll deliver the message personally that I've returned and am eager to brandish my sword." He raced for the steps, shouting over his shoulder, "He wishes a fight, John, and he shall have it."

"Take care, brother."

"Always."

* * * *

A horn sounded with a chilling blast and Marie wedged out the window to get a good look. Shouts boomed from the courtyard, and men swarmed the area. More than twenty warriors mounted their horses while an equal number raced down the trail to the sea-gate. Archie led, with a redheaded lad sprinting beside him. Archie skidded to a stop on the slippery landing, caught the boy's arm and said something to him. The lad nodded and ran back toward the castle while Archie leapt into the birlinn.

They set sail, the stormy breeze speeding them out of the bay. Clutching the windowsill, her nails scraped into the stone. Dust plumed below as mounted men galloped out the gate and headed north toward Jura. MacLean territory. The horn must have been a warning, and a bad one considering the number of men now at arms.

"Marie." A knock sounded.

"'Tis Mary MacDonald. Archie sent word for me to check on you as he left."

"Coming." A jumble of nerves bounced in her tummy as she opened the door.

The young woman wore a billowy burgundy gown, her hair

a riot of red-gold curls. The waist-length locks swayed forward over her distended belly.

"Oh my goodness. Please, sit." So many questions raged through her mind, she barely knew where to start. "What's happening? Where did Archie go?"

"Aye, thank you. My feet need a resting. Archie's sailed to answer the warning." She waddled into the room, pulled out the chair wedged under the desk and plopped down. "Dinnae fear though. My brother may be a thorn in our sides, but Lachlan cannae breach these walls. Archie and John will no' allow it."

"Will Archie come back soon?"

"Once he's seen to the threat. The guardsman who gave me Archie's message said you were fae, and he made a wish and pulled you from the circle. You're here to aid him in bringing an end to this war."

"That's right. Archie did make a wish, one I have to see through in order to return to my sister. Although as I told Archie, I'm not fae."

"Ye do sound of another world, but fae it must be." She gazed at her coat. "Even the white woolen weave you wear is so pure in color. 'Tis quite magical."

"Right." She rubbed her sleeve. The coat had cost her a pretty penny, but at least they thought her fae and not a witch. Being burnt at the stake wasn't an option. She shuddered. No, that couldn't happen. Still, at some point in time she'd have to find a way to impart the truth, in the best way she could.

"We need your magic." Mary nodded as if trying to reassure her. "I'm glad you're here."

"I'll do everything I can to help." This was the woman who'd bequeathed her the amulet. Mary too was both a MacLean and a MacDonald as she was. She lowered to her knees and gripped Mary's hands. Her ancestor was real, and right here before her. "For so long I've wanted to know more about you, why you would—" Okay, she probably shouldn't rush into this.

She needed to take care considering this time period, and Mary's condition.

Frowning, Mary leaned forward. "You've wanted to know more about what? Please, speak freely. Whatever I can do to aid the fae, I will."

"Let me show you something first. That might help a little." She tugged Mary to the window. If you look, you'll see your amulet lying on the center stone in the circle. I came through the circle, although not from his time. I'm not a witch or a fae, but from the future. You gifted your amulet to me, and you had it passed down along your eldest daughter's line until it once again came into a MacLean's possession."

Her frown deepened. "Nay. Why would I do such a thing?"

"You left instructions for me to return the amulet to Islay, to this place right here. My father was born from Lachlan MacLean's paternal line, one of his youngest sons. I received your talisman on my twenty-first birthday."

Mary's blue eyes, the same shade as hers and Katherine's, softened. "Marie, there is no future until it arrives." She squeezed her hands. "I'd no' hurt one of the fae. You need only speak the truth with me."

Mary clearly couldn't conceive the possibility any more than Archie had. Time travel and coming from the future wasn't something she'd believe either if the positions were reversed. Still, she'd keep pressing, but slow and easy. Maybe in time they'd see she spoke the truth.

Mary rubbed her swollen belly. "The bairn kicks strong this eve."

"When is your baby due?"

"A month, mayhap less. This one shall be a boy and as strong as his father." Her gaze drifted out the window. "Angus will return, and whatever I can do to aid you with Archie's wish, you need only ask."

Knowledge was power, and Mary had been the one to bring

her back to the past. "I've studied this time, but records weren't exactly well-kept. More often than not, only major events drew an actual recording, and even those were open to the writer's interpretation. Legends were passed down from family members, but again they could be skewered in the teller's favor. Will you tell me about this feud and Lachlan MacLean?"

"My, my. The fae have a strange way of speaking. Studied this time? Legends? We are in the present, my dear."

Which was fifteen-hundred and ninety. "Can you tell me how this feud between the clans started?"

"Aye. 'Twas five years past. Donald MacDonald sailed here to visit Angus. They're brothers and quite close." She eased onto the end of Archie's massive bed covered with a brown and blue wool patchwork blanket then patted the spot beside her.

"I've heard of the Chief of Sleat." She joined Mary. "He's a tough warrior."

"As are all the chiefs of these Western Isles." She clasped her hands. "Afore Donald and his men arrived here, they were forced to take shelter in Jura as a storm passed through. That's when our troubles began. Donald landed on my brother's portion of the isle, and in the dead of night, he and his men were viciously attacked by Lachlan and his warriors."

"Why would Lachlan attack when they were only seeking shelter?"

"Terreagh MacDonald had a grudge against Donald, and that night he used Donald's arrival on Lachlan's land to his advantage."

"One of your own clan betrayed their chief?" And to a MacLean no less.

"Aye, 'twas Terreagh who carried off with some of Lachlan's cattle, then turned coat and informed Lachlan it had been Donald's doing."

"How bad was the attack?"

"Donald lost sixty men. Many were sleeping when the

MacLeans snuck into camp. 'Twas a terrible slaughter."

"But Donald survived?" Clearly, he had since he was now imprisoned in Edinburgh.

"Donald remained aboard his galley. He'd taken the sea watch so his men could get their rest. He had no knowledge of the battle until 'twas done."

"Did he retaliate?" Her heart sank. Highlanders would never allow such a killing to go unpaid. That much she'd learnt from history.

"First he took his slain warriors home. Angus heard about what had happened and visited Donald at Dunscaith Castle. He hoped to intervene, but Donald intended his revenge. To try to settle the issue, Angus detoured on his way home and paid a call on my brother at Duart Castle on Mull. Lachlan though wouldnae be swayed, no' when things had always been so on edge between them. Lachlan threw Angus into his dungeons then demanded he handover his lands in the Rhinns."

"The Rhinns on this isle's west coast?" It was a sweep of land where wildlife thrived. She and Katherine had intended to visit there.

"Aye, near Loch Gruinart. To ensure Angus complied, my brother demanded my eldest son, James, be held as his hostage until the land transfer was complete. My bairn was five at the time. I had to send my son away, and 'twas only after I did that Angus was released." Tears welled as she twisted her hands in her lap.

"I'm so sorry." She rubbed Mary's back. "What of James?"

"When Angus asked Lachlan to meet him at Mullintrea near the Rhinns to sign the transfer parchments, Lachlan used James as leverage. Angus knew Lachlan would never hand James over, no' even after the deed was signed."

"What did Angus do?"

"Lachlan is still my brother, and Angus was well aware Lachlan felt guilt with my marriage to him being an arranged one." She stood and paced the room. "Angus demanded Lachlan settle their differences with honor. He treated Lachlan well for the day, but once Lachlan and his men retired to the village for the night, Angus and his warriors surrounded their longhouse. He wanted James back and knew I was becoming more distraught."

"I can't believe the extent of this feud, or that an innocent child was involved."

"My brother even tried to use James as a shield. Thankfully Angus cornered him, and Lachlan finally surrendered."

"What of James now?"

"He carries the scars of his trialing time, as well as a burning hatred for his uncle." Tears trailed down her cheeks and she dashed them away. "Angus spared my brother's life that night so as not to escalate the feud, though he did take the life of Terreagh MacDonald who was among Lachlan's men. In the years since, Lachlan has continued to seek his revenge. He's ravaged our land where he could, while Angus has plundered in return. All in the isles have felt the effects of this war."

Poor Mary. She'd been caught right in the middle, her amulet a heavy reminder she was both MacDonald and MacLean. Two great clans at war. "What can you tell me about your amulet? I know so little about it."

"Angus had it made and gifted to me on my wedding day. 'Twas supposed to represent the joining of both clans although that has never been achieved. I wear it because 'tis a firm reminder I belong to both. Lachlan is still my brother, and as much as I hate what he's done, he's kin. I wish Angus had no' been taken by the king, nor Donald."

What a mess. How on earth was she supposed to fix this, a feud of such massive proportions? Stupid fae. Those little folk had a lot to answer for.

"Were you aware of the king's missive? That he wished for all three chiefs to make amends for their actions."

"Angus never spoke of any such thing."

"Is there anyone other than the king who could sort this feud?"

"Nay. Lachlan fights to win, and now he remains the sole aggressor. On the loose, I'm no' sure what he'll do."

An ache settled between her eyes and she rubbed it. Three chiefs and a king, and she had to keep history on course. Adventure didn't even begin to come close to describing her current mission. "Archie seems prepared to fight."

"Neither he nor John will allow Islay to fall, nor Lachlan to live if it's within their power." Mary brushed her fingers over Marie's brow. "I've burdened you enough for this eve. We should speak more in the morn. Would some rest aid you in sorting your thoughts?"

"Traveling back to my own time certainly would." Though she doubted it would happen any time soon. "Thank you. You've given me much to consider. You should rest too. Will you be able to speak to me tomorrow?"

"Of course. Sleep well, Marie." Mary closed the door behind her.

She leaned against the windowsill. The circle was clear, and she was here to stay. "Katherine, this adventure right now sucks, but stay safe. I'll see to Archie's wish, somehow and someway." She blew a kiss. "Then I'll get back to you. I promise I will."

Yes, it was a promise she'd never break.

* * * *

Feet braced wide, Archie gripped the birlinn's ropes alongside Eric, one of his best warriors. The storm had filled the sails and this close to the shore 'twas necessary to keep a tight rein on their direction to ensure they didn't go aground.

MacLean would pay if he were behind the current attack, which he didn't doubt. Once he found MacLean, he'd make certain the man understood he'd never be laird over any portion of Islay. 'Twas MacDonald land, and no one else's.

He'd given James his promise as the lad had raced after him to the sea-gate. His father would be returned to him, right after he'd disposed of his treacherous uncle. James was strong. He'd survived a tortuous abduction and come through it. Once the boy became a man, he'd aid his father in leading their clan, and he'd make a fine warrior, one Angus would be proud of. For now though, Islay was under his care, and he wouldn't fail his chief, or Mary.

"Do you smell that, Captain?" George kept a look out from the bow.

The salty scent of the sea tickled his nose, and there, a hint of smoke. They were almost at Ardbeg where Will remained on guard. He turned the sail a touch and caught more wind. These past five years, MacLean had taken every opportunity to pillage and burn their lands, but he'd never gotten this close to Dunyvaig. MacLean may have heard of Angus's imprisonment, or if not, he was taking his chances at striking so nearby. "To the village," he called to his men. "With haste."

Muscles flexed, he wrestled with the ropes as the waves churned. The scent of smoke thickened as they rounded the tip.

"Look, Captain!" George motioned toward land.

A thick, ashy plume smothered the horizon. Ardbeg burned. They had to move faster. Longhouses blazed, and his people formed a living line from the burning buildings to the water's edge. Each swung a pail, one to the other.

"Oars," he bellowed as he dropped the sail and bounded to the bow. They crested the waves and fifteen feet from the rocky shoreline, he leapt over the side and landed hip-deep in the water. He shoved through then jogged toward Will.

"Captain." Will jabbed a hand toward the forest path. "MacLean's men snuck in like the cowards they are, attacked and left the winds to fan the flames. I would have made chase, but all hands are needed here."

A woman blackened with grimy soot carried a bairn toward

the line and joined her kinsmen. They damn well better not have lost any lives. "We save the village first." He signaled to his men as they bounded onto land. "The fires must go out. Aid as you can."

Everything within him raged to go after MacLean. Instead, he strode across to the woman, swung her bairn onto his shoulders and joined in the battle to save what they could. "Hold on, young one. MacLean willnae win this day."

"Fire bad." The child wrapped pudgy arms around his neck. "Men bad."

"Aye, they'll be brought to justice." He hefted the next pail along. Marie's magic wouldn't go amiss. Some rain wouldn't either. If only those storm clouds would release their burden. Lifting his face to the skies, he sent his wish free.

A fat drop splashed his cheek then another landed on his nose.

The heavens opened and the rains came. Aye, his faerie was a magical charm he'd wish for again should he have need.

All around his kinsmen cheered, hands lifted to the sky. They waited for the rain to work its wonder. Slowly the flames hissed and died.

Drenched, he called out, "No MacLean will ever dishearten us. We rally together."

MacLean would be held accountable for this destruction.

He'd make certain of it.

Chapter 3

"Load the cart with whatever we can spare." A booming male voice filtered through the window.

Marie jerked awake on the soft mattress, scrubbed her gritty eyes and climbed out of the covers. She was still in the past and Archie hadn't returned. Hopping across to the window, she tugged on her white leather boots. Dawn pierced the horizon, casting a silvery-pink hue over the loch. After last night's torrential downpour, the skies had finally cleared and the grassy moors glistened.

The circle looked no different this morning, her amulet still lying untouched across the center stone. Katherine hadn't come. Her heart heaved for her sister. No, she had to remain strong. She had a wish to see to so she could return through time, and she couldn't do that without the man who'd made the wish in the first place.

"We're almost there, George. The cook will bring the loaves of bread she's prepared and ye can set out." John stood below in the courtyard, one hand braced against the wooden sides of a cart overflowing with blankets, clothing and tools.

His voice had first woken her.

Two lads dashed from the side entrance and tucked armfuls

of bread into the rear of the cart.

John clapped the driver on the back. "Inform Archie I'll have another score of men there my midday." John had the same dark hair with a hint of gold on the shoulder-length ends as Archie. The strands swept across his claymore holstered snugly over his back. These warriors were always armed.

A gangly boy wearing breeches two inches too short raced out of the keep. "John." He'd chased Archie to the sea-gate the night before. He had Mary's bright red-gold locks, although cut close to his head. "I'm coming to the village. They're my people too. Father would expect me to do what I can."

"The fire was extinguished by the rains, James. You need to remain with your mother. With your father gone, she worries about you."

"Mother wishes to come too. Archie has no' forbid it."

Indecision crossed John's face then he slowly nodded. "George said MacLean was nowhere to be found once the men completed their search. You'll have a strong guard. Inform your mother she may—"

"He need no' inform me. I'm right here." Mary bustled out of the keep with furs draped over her arms. "I've sent a maid to awaken Marie. As Archie's faerie, she too should come."

"Allow me." John heaved the furs from her arms and tossed them into the cart. "You're no' to overdo things, and you're to return when Archie says."

"Aye, whatever you say." A sneaky smile lifted her lips before she quickly straightened them, one very reminiscent of Katherine's cheeky smile. Clasping her blue woolen skirts, she clambered in beside the driver.

The maid hadn't yet arrived, but she didn't want to miss that cart. Where Archie was, she needed to be. Out the door, she raced through the dimly lit corridor and down the winding stairwell. Archie hadn't brought her in from this direction, but the side stairs. Hopefully these led out.

She pounced off the last step, rounded a corner and weaved through the great hall where beautiful landscape tapestries hung on the stone walls. Above the blazing fireplace, a massive two-handed great sword encrusted with precious stones, glinted. She rounded the trestle tables and whizzed past the elevated dais.

At the door, a maid swept the floor while another shooed a dog outside.

"Excuse me." She ran outside and across the stony courtyard to the cart.

"There you are, my dear. Come." Mary waved.

She scrambled onto the front seat next to Mary. "I heard from my window. MacLean's attack was in the village then?"

"Aye, but the rains doused the flames, lessening the loss. There is still much to be done though. The luck of the faeries is needed this day." She motioned toward John. "Have you met Archie's brother?"

"Not formally, just from beyond the veil." She pressed out her hand. "Nice to meet you, John."

"'Tis a pleasure to meet one of the fae. What a shame it wasnae I who pulled you from the circle." He lifted her hand to his lips, kissed her knuckles and released her. "Spin your magic for us, Marie. We must ensure MacLean never infiltrates our shores again."

"I'll do what I can. Was anyone hurt?" She smoothed the wrinkles from her white woolen coat.

"No lives were lost as the warning went out in time. Give aid where you can, and travel safely." He turned to the half dozen warriors mounted on horseback. "Guard Mary and Archie's faerie well."

The driver tugged the reins and the cart jolted forward over the stony path. James ran and clambered onto the pelts in the back while two warriors rode out the arched gate ahead of them.

The remaining men on horseback took positions at their side and rear.

"I'm glad we're going, Mary. I can't work any magic if I sit on the sidelines." Bounced about, she grasped the bench. "This is a rather refreshing form of travel. I never thought I'd see Scotland quite this way."

"What other forms do the fae use?"

"Rather spectacular sorts." But less about that. She had to focus on her mission. "Is Archie certain it was MacLean who attacked?"

"Aye, I'm afraid so." Mary patted her leg. "My brother would rid himself of my entire MacDonald clan in order to rule Islay. This attack is just another of many."

"I hate Uncle." James spat over the side of the cart. "One day I'll be a warrior as Father is and hurt Uncle like he's hurt us."

"Careful how you speak, James." Mary sucked in a long breath then leaned in and whispered, "James is but ten, any childhood he had taken from him."

So sad. Children grew up far too fast in this time, and danger lurked where it shouldn't.

The cart rattled down the trail to the north. They skimmed the edge of the forest until the coastline forced them to veer through the thick woods.

A guardsman raised a hand, called a halt, and the driver eased back on the reins and stopped.

"Wait here," the warrior instructed him. "I'll track ahead along the forest path and ensure all is well."

The horses whinnied and the guardsmen behind them brought their mounts closer, offering their protection from every side.

"Dinnae fear, Marie. George is one of our best trackers." Shielding her eyes against the sun's glare, Mary eyed the coast. "Lachlan will have retreated knowing Archie will have warriors searching for him. My brother is a strategist and will wait for the right time to pounce again. I'm certain."

"I've never experienced anything like this before." She relaxed a little, easing against the backboard as Mary did. The sky was a soft blue, clear except for a wisp or two of cloud, and ahead, the warrior George, disappeared within the beautiful elm and ash trees. "It's hard to believe such destruction lies in wait for us. How long until we get there?"

"'Tis a short journey, no more than a league, and George willnae take long. John will have warriors on the lookout within the forest too."

She had no idea what a league was, but it didn't sound far.

A pretty chirpy bird whistle broke the stillness. The driver snapped the horses' reins and they moved on.

"George didn't come back."

"Aye, but 'twas his call." Mary stroked her belly. "George will ride a furlong or two ahead. 'Tis his way."

The warriors took every precaution, and Marie's need to see Archie soon buzzed strongly through her. Within the faerie circle, she'd connected with him as if more than his wish tied them together. She was meant to be here, this adventure hers. She'd embrace it. Katherine would want her to, as much as she'd want her to hurry and return home.

"Where do you live?" Mary lengthened her legs and wriggled her toes. "I'm curious to learn more."

"Near the ocean, at a place known as the Gold Coast." She snatched an amber falling leaf as it fluttered past. "It's spring back home, and the land is lush and green."

"The fae live back-to-front then, and along a coast of gold. How intriguing." She smiled at James. "Marie is fae, and there is a coast of gold where she lives. So many riches. Can you imagine?"

"Is that how the faeries get their gold?" James scrambled closer then propped his chin in his upturned palms.

"No, I meant I live along a coast with golden sand. That's why it's called the Gold Coast. My twin sister, Katherine, loves to swim there as I do. On our thirteenth birthday, our mother presented us with diving lessons on the coast and we explored its beautiful reefs. Definitely no gold, or at least I never saw any."

"Lessons?" James's blue eyes sparkled. "'Tis easy enough to duck your head, toss your feet in the air and dive. Why would one need lessons?"

"Cheeky." She flicked his arm. "The lessons were required because diving around the coral reefs takes great care. Our instructor gave Katherine and me a mask. It's placed over the eyes and mouth and has a clear, ah, front."

"Water does no' leak in?" James edged up higher, completely intrigued.

"Nope. The mask suctions to the face so when one dives you have a perfect view of the reef and sea-life. During our lessons, Mum waited on the boat, but before long she was in the water, chasing to catch us up. I'll never forget holding hands with her and Katherine as we dived. There's such beauty in the wild depths. I loved it."

"We dinnae have such masks. That is some fae magic." Mary nodded at James. "Would you enjoy diving in such a way?"

"Aye." He grinned. "Marie, could you weave some of your magic and take me diving as you did?"

"The magic was Mum's gift. I can't wield such unless I took you with me to the Gold Coast."

Gasping, he gawked at Mary. "Can—"

"Nay, you are no' leaving me with your father away." She wagged a finger at him.

"Once he returns then, Mother?"

"You'll be fostered after the winter and already I miss you. I think no'."

"I can't take you anyway, James. I live too far away. Even I can't get back, or at least not until I've seen to Archie's wish." They emerged from the forest and the sun warmed her through.

She shrugged her coat off and straightened the long sleeves of her white blouse.

"Oh, such a sheer fabric." Mary fingered the silk. "'Tis as beautiful as your coat. How do the fae weave this fine a thre—"

A horse galloped over the rise toward them. George circled their party, calling out, "All remains clear. Archie awaits our arrival."

James bounced onto his bottom. "I want to do everything I can to help."

"We all do." Mary squeezed his hand. "Your father would be proud of all you've taken on at the keep lately. Cleaning the armorer's tools, sweeping out the stalls, helping me with the young ones. No task goes unnoticed. "

They crested the rise and the wind blew Marie's blond hair across her face. She tucked the flyaway strands behind her ears. A beautiful wide stretch of sparkling blue sea lay before them. A few fishing skiffs bobbed beyond the breakers, and the birlinn Archie had sailed away in, rocked where anchored near the water's edge.

The village lay spread within the bay's basin and up along the rising moors scattered with rocks. Where the grass grew thick, children played tag, and to the side of the trail they followed, a dozen or more bare-chested men heaved the ashy remains of someone's home into a clumpy pile.

Their guardsmen veered toward the stables and two stable hands rushed out to take their mounts.

"There's Archie." James jumped from the back of the cart and raced alongside them.

Archie stood alone on an exposed beam at the top of a longhouse away from the others, his bare back glistening with sweat. He walked across the arched wooden slab, and in the center, slammed one foot down as if testing its strength.

The driver stopped the cart near him. He offered Mary a hand and she nodded her thanks as she hopped down.

Marie slowly stood and smiled at her Highland warrior. His body was hard and packed with muscle, his shoulders and arms thick and strong. His chest held the finest smattering of hair, the same color as the dark brown of his head. Oh, and below the planes of his glorious chest, his abs, layer upon tight layer, rippled as he tested another cross beam.

"Down with you." Mary tapped her leg. "We have a cart to unload."

"One second." She wiped her drooling mouth. Archie's powerful form was magnificent. She'd certainly like to get more up close and personal with him. "Hey, Mr. Wish Maker," she called out. "Be careful up there."

His gaze flew toward her then down her body. Deep frown lines formed across his brow as if he'd assessed her dress not up to standard. Without her coat, her pants were far more obvious. Women didn't don such clothing in this age, but her loosely styled slacks should still be acceptable.

"Dinnae move. I'll be right there," he muttered. Or maybe they weren't acceptable.

"I heard you might need a touch of magic."

"Aye, always." He strode to the end of the beam at the side of the house, crinkled up his leather pants at the knee and jumped. His booted feet thumped on the ground and lifted scattered ash into the air.

The man was too impressive by far. She cleared her throat. "You shouldn't leap from buildings. You're not Spider—no, never mind."

"It was a mere hop." He grasped her waist and swung her down beside him.

"This longhouse looks okay."

"It's structurally sound and will only require re-thatching. Three homes though will need to be rebuilt." He lifted a brow toward Mary. "Did you journey well?"

"'Twas good for me to get some air, and my clan need me."

She toddled past him with a smile. "I'll go and help where I can."

"I'd expect naught less." He jerked his head toward James. "Go fetch the midwife and have her keep an eye on your mother. Once that's done, find Will and he'll assign you a task."

"Aye, Captain." He dashed away.

"And you. Come with me." He caught her hand and tugged her along behind him into the building. "Lass, explain yourself. Why can I see right through your blouse?"

* * * *

Never had Archie expected his faerie to be wearing such sheer clothing under her coat. A lacy chemise covered her, but not nearly enough for his liking.

"It's just the fabric." She plucked the silk away from her skin. "I'm decent underneath, and this clothing is quite respectable where I come from."

"I dinnae care for it. My men's thoughts will wander with you dressed this way. Mine are." He fingered her locks, a cascade that touched her waist. The sun's rays through the open roof feasted on her, setting the white and gold strands ablaze. "'Tis far too suggestive."

"Well, you're not even wearing a shirt. You can hardly call this blouse suggestive when all I can see is your bare skin." She licked her lips as she ran her gaze over his chest. "My thoughts are definitely wandering."

"Take care, Marie." He should not be so fascinated with his faerie, not when she was here to grant his wish and no more. However, he couldn't halt himself from inching closer to her. "Since you arrived with Mary, I take it you've spoken to her."

"We spoke at length last night. She told me all that's happened these past five years between your clan and MacLean's. I was aware the blood feuds ran rampant, but not the exact reasons why. I have a far better understanding now, although I could use more knowledge. What can you tell me?"

"That I intend to set out after MacLean."

"More retribution?"

"'Tis the only way. MacLean does no' listen to reason. Angus's attempt to speak with him at the beginning only escalated the feud."

"So Mary said." She nibbled her lower lip. Such deep concentration crossed her face. "I agree MacLean hasn't the ability to listen. Although it's strange I've read about him being an accomplished chief. He certainly warred, but he was always good to his people."

"Were he no' good to his people, he'd no' have remained their chief." He thumbed her velvety lips, and wished her lacy undergarments were now a touch thinner. Damn, he'd have to do something about her clothing. Her white breeches clung to her legs, outlining every single delectable inch of them. Beautifully shaped, and for his eyes alone. Nay, not his. What was he thinking? He snagged his shirt from the center beam and dragged it over her head. It swamped her to her knees and covered all on display. "Dinnae take that off."

"Is my shirt really that big of an issue?" She lifted the collar over her nose and inhaled. "Oh, you smell good, like a fresh ocean breeze. Maybe I won't mind wearing this after all."

He groaned, his groin tightening. His faerie was a temptress, and it had been far too long since he'd bedded a woman. What would she feel like—hell, he needed to get his blasted thoughts under control. "A fresh breeze, aye. Highlanders live on the water. 'Tis how we travel around the isles."

"In my time"—she lifted one delicately arched eyebrow—"we travel through the air as well. One can board a plane. It takes off and flies across the sky."

"I see your imagination still runs rife." The fae loved to play their games and this lass was no different. Tempting, enchanting, and his to care for. He'd taken on quite the task, but thus far, enjoyable.

"Or it could be the truth if you would but see it." She slowly circled him, running her finger along his skin at the waist of his trews. "Where I come from, man no longer travels by horse, but within large steel contraptions that roll on wheels. Although do you want to hear something truly wicked?"

"Nay." His thoughts were bad enough.

"Boats are made of steel, and they don't simply sail across the sea, but also cruise the depths below. They're called submarines, and they're fully enclosed."

"Now I know you lie." Although seductively. Such travel would allow one to sneak up on their enemy. He liked.

"And what if I'm telling the truth?" She sidled around until they stood face to face. "Ask me a question, anything you'd like."

"How do these submarines rise from the depths? The concept is intriguing, albeit impossible."

"They have tanks which draw water in to allow them to fall below the waterline, and once it's time to go up, engines pump the water back out. Engines you won't see for hundreds of years." She trailed a finger down the center of his chest. "My thoughts are still wandering."

"You play with fire, my faerie." He captured her hands and draped them around his neck. "I like it too much."

"And you're a challenge, one which I like too much."

"Do you wish to test the waters between us? Dare me and we shall." Aye, he was up for a dare, and he hoped she was too.

* * * *

Marie should step back, but for the life of her, she couldn't. Instead, she slid her fingers through his silky brown hair and stroked his scalp. "I dare you. I'm a twenty-first century woman, whether you believe me or not. And we play by a whole separate set of rules."

"So you wish to play as the fae do?" He lowered his head to

the curve of her neck and brushed his lips over her flesh. "Say aye. I need to hear your agreement plain and clear."

"Yes, bring on the fire. Set as many challenges as you like." She tipped her head to the side and he trailed his lips lower.

"Fire it is then." He settled his mouth over her pulse and sucked, hard.

Her knees wobbled, and she latched onto his shoulders. "Um, nice start."

"Nice? Your heartbeat flutters like the wings of a bird." He pressed every inch of his body against hers, and heat raced the entire length. "I want to kiss you."

Well, that she really didn't mind. This adventure surely wouldn't hurt with some kissing involved. "If you wish."

"I wish." He covered her mouth with his, and the taste of him swarmed her senses. Oh, yes. Adventure was good. Wanting more, she kissed him back, molding her mouth to his.

"You taste so sweet." He licked over her lower lip with the most seductive stroke. Desire bolted through her. Then he caressed her sides, roamed down and scooped her bottom up. Lifted higher, he pressed himself hard against her, and he was hard.

Sweet heaven. Keeping hold, she seized his powerful biceps. "I really like you without the shirt."

"I really like you with mine on." Then he kissed her deeper, until their breath mingled as one. "How much fire can you handle? I need to touch you."

"You already have a good hold on—" He cupped her breast and thumbed the peak. "Oh, okay. I'm good with that too."

"You said you play by a separate set of rules. If this is unacceptable, say so." His golden eyes swam with desire, and there wasn't a chance she wanted to snuff that out.

"You won't hear me say stop." Why had she never experienced an attraction like this before? Not that she'd actually had much experience with men. She and Katherine had spent years nursing Mum through her illness. Cancer was brutal, and being with Mum had been their priority, not men. Relationships could wait, whereas Mum couldn't. "I really like your brand of fire, Archie."

Yes, she was prepared to play with whatever fire he wielded.

* * * *

Archie groaned as Marie pressed her breast more fully into his palm. From the moment she'd arrived at the village, he'd wanted to cover her up, and now he wished for the exact opposite.

He stroked the pebbled peak of her nipple. Her breast was lush, and he ached for a closer touch. Surely, no harm could come from it. He swept the collar aside then eased his hand inside. The lacy chemise slid sensuously over the back of his hand as he filled his palm with her warm flesh.

Heat surged into his loins and he returned to her mouth. He plunged his tongue inside and drank in her sweet nectar. 'Twas a losing battle to keep his passion in check, and even more so when she entwined her tongue with his and drove him beyond his endurance in a delicious dance.

More. He wanted more, and not just to have his hand against her. He had to taste her. He eased the shirt over her shoulder and licked her nipple. Perfect. He rolled his tongue around the peak and sucked.

"Archie." She moaned and curved into him. "That feels sooo good."

"Aye, delicious." He gave her other breast equal attention. He lapped the tight bud, gorging himself on the faerie he'd wished for.

"Captain?"

Hell. Will's voice penetrated the fog in his head. Pulling back, he fought for a breath.

"Don't stop." Marie clutched his shoulders, her eyes hazed

with desire.

"I must. One of my men approaches."

"What?" She gasped and yanked up her shirt. "I didn't hear him."

"We're no' done." He dropped a quick kiss on her lips. "No' by half."

A fire now raged, and his faerie had enflamed him.

Damn his man for intruding.

Chapter 4

Her Highlander could certainly kiss. Marie fanned her face as Archie guided her outside. What an enticing mission she had ahead, and in more ways than one.

"There ye are, Captain." Will tramped toward them. "We have everything we need to begin work on the walls."

"Good. The beams on this one are sound. Allow me to introduce Marie."

"Good morn, my lady." Will bobbed his head.

"Nice to meet you." She moved toward him, but Archie stepped in front of her as though she shouldn't trust his man.

"Marie is under my protection. Inform all the men 'tis so." He crossed his arms, and his back muscles rippled.

"Aye, Captain. Word has already spread of your faerie, although I'll pass your instructions along."

"Has the patrol returned with aught more?"

"There's still no sign of MacLean. He likely arrived from the sea then left the same way. I do though bring a message to the lady from Mary."

"Speak it."

"Mary's down on the beach. She asked Marie to join her."

She eased around Archie. "Thanks. Message received. It's

truly nice to meet you."

"You're welcome, and 'tis nice to meet you." Whistling, he strode away.

Archie continued to watch Will, not turning. "Mary isnae the only one who holds deep knowledge of MacLean. Ask me what you wish of the scourge."

"How soon do you expect MacLean to return? To attack again." She hooked a finger into his waistband and tugged.

He spun around, caught her hand. "Knowing we'll seek our revenge, he'll fortify his defenses against us first. 'Tis a deadly game we play, one he knows well."

"He fights for his clan, as you fight for yours. There must be a way around all this warring."

"Angus attempted to speak to MacLean at the beginning of this feud and his brother-in-law wouldnae listen. Instead, the feud exploded. The MacLean chief must die in order for us to win this war, and I intend to see the deed done, with the aid of your magic."

"I never promised to aid you in killing him." Not caring for that idea at all, she tugged her hand free. "After touring the ruins of Dunyvaig, Katherine and I intended to visit MacLean's marker. A monument was erected in the churchyard of Kilchoman, close to where he died in battle. Although it doesn't happen for several years yet."

"You're saying he dies? At Kilchoman?" He scrubbed a hand along his jaw. "That's on the west of Islay near Loch Gruinart. Had MacLean died on our land then his men would have taken his remains and buried him at Duart Castle on the Isle of Mull. No warrior leaves his chief behind."

"The battle was grave. It took him, and many of his men."

"Tell me the date of this battle."

"If I did, will you believe I'm from the future?" Maybe she was finally getting somewhere.

"Nay. You're fae, but mayhap have the sight."

Did he mean foresight? Great. What would it take to make him believe? She tapped her sides. "And here I thought we were about to make some inroads. Well, I can't recall the exact date, but it's before the turn of the century."

"I willnae wait another decade to see to MacLean's death."

"Too bad, because I won't change history so you can kill him any earlier. I have to bring about a resolution to this war, not encourage it."

"His death is assured. You cannae halt me from seeing to that."

"MacLean is young and still fathering his children. Should you kill him before his time, my paternal line might be extinguished before it even begins. I'm a MacLean, remember? Not good for me." Yes, and since she had no intention of dying before she'd even been born, he had to concede.

"You're no' from the future."

"We are not going back there again." The man was impossible, and they could probably go in circles with this conversation. She had to uncover a way to make him believe her, which she would. Somehow. "Let's move on for now. Why don't you tell me more about the Rhinns. Mary said that particular piece of land is in dispute."

"Aye, but it still belongs to the MacDonalds."

Sure, he'd say that. He was a MacDonald, which meant maybe Mary was the only one here partial to conveying the full and honest truth. "Angus MacDonald was taken by the king's men because of his fight with MacLean. I need you to think about winning this war without causing his death. In my time, wars are fought and people lose their lives far too often. I want to use my magic to its best advantage, ensuring a change for the better, not worse. What about the king? It's James VI, right?"

"Aye, 'tis he."

"He was known as one of the greatest kings in history. He certainly has my vote for fixing this. Surely he holds the most impartial view of all."

"The king willnae be permitted to rule us. Our form of fighting has served us well and we have no intention of changing it."

"Ah-huh, and you also need to keep an open mind. Your wish brought me here, so now let me do what I'm supposed to and impart some magic, in the form of knowledge. What happens if the king is right in the way he's addressing this situation? He wants to bring all three chiefs involved in this feud together, to settle this dispute by ensuring they atone for their actions. A sound move if you ask me." She paced back and forth. "Archie, peace should always prevail over war."

"I want MacLean's death, no' his imprisonment at the king's hands."

"And I'd like a fighting chance to live." She had to make him look past his absolute need for death. "You can't kill the man who's yet to father my paternal line. It's not going to happen on my watch."

"It will, and since you're no' from the future, 'tis a moot point you argue."

"You want to take that risk? Condemn me to death?"

His gaze hardened "You stand afore me. His death willnae cause yours as you already live. MacLean must be held accountable for his continued attacks."

"I get that part." Yet all three chiefs needed to undergo the same accountability. For now, they'd have to disagree, until she could really work some magic on him. Obstinate man. "Can we talk about Will and your men? Do I need to take care for some reason?"

"Nay." He frowned something fierce. "Why would you even ask?"

"You warned Will to pass along your message. Then you shielded me from him. I got the impression there might be a problem."

"Will enjoys the lasses too much, and you're no' his to enjoy." He glanced toward the bay. "The fishermen have come in. Mary and the women will need aid with preparing the meal. Ensure she does no' overtax herself."

Near the water's edge, the fishermen knelt before flat stones, cleaning their catch. A lad whose loose-legged breeches were hitched with a thin belt at his waist, heaved a pail of fish as he trudged uphill toward two white-aproned women cooking over a fire. Mary sat propped on a stone close by, her skirts spread about her as she mended a shirt.

"No problem. My mother was much like Mary, always wanting to be where help was needed. I had to curtail her movements near the end of her sickness, so she conserved her strength."

"I'm sorry about your mother, Marie." He stroked the back of her head.

"Thanks." She fought back tears as she stepped away. "I'll go look after Mary. In the meantime, you go and slap some stones and clay around and consider my point of view. That'd be really handy."

He chuckled. "Lass, you are an amusing faerie."

"Yes I am." She followed the trail toward Mary. Ahead, the women added the fresh fish the lad had brought them to the bubbling pot.

"There you are." Mary extended a hand toward the rock next to her. "You and Archie appeared to be in a deep discussion."

"He's determined to kill MacLean."

"Aye, my brother's been a thorn in his side for years."

"But he wants his death."

Mary's blue eyes misted. "I understand, even though I'm saddened to say so."

"Tell me more about MacLean. If I'm to work my magic, I need as much information about him as you can give me."

"Lachlan was my father's only son, his heir and successor." She slid her needle through the shirt, repairing a hole. "My sisters and I adored him, although Lachlan grew up well afore his time since Father passed when he was only fifteen."

"Are you saying he was still a minor when he had to lead his clan?"

"Aye, but we called him Big Lachlan. Fifteen he may have been, but no one could miss him in a crowd, no' when he towered over them all. His skills were immense, and he excelled with the sword."

"What of his mind?" A seagull squawked as it circled overhead. It followed the lad swinging his pail as he dashed back toward the fishermen.

"Naught ever slipped his notice, no' from the beginning." She looked skyward with a shake of her head. "He's a strategist, as Father never was. Father enjoyed his pleasures and burdened our clan with large debts in his five years as chief. Lachlan wars as he does in order to return to our clan all Father lost. The boy I knew disappeared when he became our clan's chief."

"I've read—I mean, doesn't he have some redeeming qualities? He can't be all bad."

"Aye. He loves his people, except he's ruthless in his endeavors. I fear these past five years have hardened him beyond reproach. His actions certainly speak so, and there's nay telling what he'll do next."

"What of his family?"

"He wed Lady Margaret, the Earl of Glencairn's daughter afore our feud began. They have bairns."

"Which makes him how old?"

"Two and thirty."

She tapped her fingers on her knees. He was too young to die. Even the turn of the century was too soon. Archie simply couldn't go after MacLean, a decision her Highlander had already made. She'd definitely need a ton of magic to sort this.

"What worries you, Marie?" Mary tucked a lock of Marie's blond hair over her shoulder. "You appear so burdened."

"Fairly much everything, and I miss my sister." The future existed, and with her here in the past, she could easily alter it if she wasn't careful. Time to cover her bases. "I need you to do something for me. I can't afford to mess up whatever magic brought me here, or the fact you bequeathed your amulet to me. I realize you don't believe I'm from the future, but please, ensure your keepsake is passed down your maternal line, to your eldest daughter and so forth, until it once again comes into the possession of a MacLean."

"'Tis a special kind of magic belonging to the fae to make such a request." Mary slowly nodded. "If that is your wish, I shall hold fast to it."

"I more than wish it." Good. One problem down. She was glad to have taken care of that necessity. She breathed deep, taking in the heavenly scent of seafood stew wafting along with the salty sea breeze. "Tell me what I can do to help, Mary."

Giggles floated toward them.

"The midday meal is almost ready." Mary seized a blanket folded at her feet and spread it out. "Oh, and there are the rest of our helpers."

Along the path, a group of girls carried the fresh loaves of bread they'd brought on the cart from Dunyvaig.

Mary nodded at the girls as they set the food down. "Go and call the men. The sooner they arrive, the sooner we can all eat."

After bobbing their heads, they raced off.

"Marie, you slice the bread and pass it out"—Mary pointed to a knife near a stack of bowls—"while I aid the ladies in serving the stew."

"Will do." She got to work.

Before long, the men arrived. Serving girls brought flagons of ale from a nearby longhouse and moved through the men as they relaxed on the grass and low boulders.

Weaving among them, Marie offered the bread.

Archie strode in and a serving girl dashed to his side and handed him a bowl of stew. Still he wore no shirt, and the girl tending him ducked her head, her cheeks flushing. He seemed oblivious to it all.

She wound around the others toward him and held out her tray. "Help yourself, but don't eat it until you've put on a shirt."

"I would but you're wearing it." His grin was wide as he swiped a thick slice of bread, dunked it in his stew, and took a hearty bite.

Her belly rumbled as he chewed.

"Have you no' eaten yet?"

"No, and I won't until you put on a shirt."

"This tastes good." He dipped his bread and held it toward her. "Come, my faerie. Take a bite."

"I'll bite you if you don't get dressed." She stalked away. The man shouldn't be showing off so much flesh, not unless she was the only one ogling the wondrous sight.

His chuckles followed her as she clomped toward the fire. Yes, those were totally irrational thoughts, but he'd kissed her, and she'd relished kissing him back. He was her Highlander, for now.

After plunking her tray down, she accepted a bowl of stew from Mary then marched along the shoreline to find a quiet spot to eat.

She was here for a reason. To perform some magic, and to get her Highlander to listen to her.

Stubborn man.

* * * *

"Here, I've mended this one." Mary tossed Archie a clean shirt. "Now behave, and go look after your faerie. She appears put out, and I've no doubt you're the cause of it."

"My thanks, Mary." He pulled the tunic over his head then followed Marie. Such a spitfire, although her frustration clearly matched his own which had ridden him hard since they'd kissed.

Past a clump of bushes, she set her stew on the grassy edge, sat and tucked the sides of his shirt under her knees. She glared at him, her lush lips tightening. Feisty too. Just how he liked his women.

"You didn't have to follow me, not unless you want to apologize."

"I apologize, and I missed your agreeable company. Did you glean any further information from Mary?" He eased in beside her.

"Yes, that you're up against a warrior chief of immense strength, both of body and mind. He's also a man I still can't allow you to kill. Now I have to find a way to convince you too, a task which would be infinitely easier if you just went along with me."

"I see." He'd never agree to her request. He stretched out and lay on his back, hands clasped behind his head. Now to make her understand his position. "You willnae succeed in swaying my mind. I know MacLean, and he'll continue to attack unless I dispose of him."

"Do you truly love to war this much?"

"'Tis my life." He'd never veer from protecting his clan and seeing to his duty.

"Life should be treasured, not tossed away." She eased onto her back next to him, sighed and stared at the sky. "If you're going to be this obstinate then so am I. When you leave for this war, I'm coming. We need to stick together."

"Nay. Our women arenae permitted to travel into battle. I need you here."

"You made your wish, and I can't aid you from a distance." She rolled onto her side and faced him. "I'm coming. You, Mr. Highlander, have met your match."

"No amount of persuasion will change my mind." But damn, he liked her tenacity.

"Persuasion doesn't even come into it."

"You're a contrary lass." A spirited woman drew him in as no other could.

"Maybe. Maybe not." She leaned in and touched her nose to his. "I have a feeling contrary women appeal to you. Am I right?"

"Resilience is a worthy attribute, but so is abiding by a man's word."

"I only cared for the first part of your answer." She kissed the tip of his nose. "You don't currently have a resilient woman do you?"

"Nay. I would no' have kissed you otherwise."

"I liked your kisses."

"Would you be agreeable if I offered more?" He wanted to take what they'd done earlier, further. He cared far more for this turn in their conversation too.

"I could be persuaded." She brushed a finger along his lower lip. "Where I come from women speak openly about these sorts of things. We also care for ourselves, ensuring we're protected."

He'd given her his word he'd protect her, unless she spoke of getting with child. Aye, that was likely it. "I would protect you against all things."

"How do you propose to do that?"

He settled a hand over her hip. "When I was old enough to understand why my mother had passed after giving birth to John and me, that she'd lost all strength from blood loss, I made a vow. I'm content with finding pleasure in a woman's body, without allowing my seed to take root."

"Oh, I'm so sorry to hear about your mother's passing." Frowning, she stroked his chest. "I've spent years with my mother, cherishing every single moment. We never knew when or if her illness would ever take her, or at least not until the end. It's awful you never even had any time with your mother."

"My brother and I were never without love. Our clan cared for us, and now we guard and protect them."

"So I see." Her gaze softened. "You are one very intriguing man. There is a soft heart under all that hard muscle."

"Nay, no' soft. Weathered and tough from the trials of time, but I find pleasure where I can." Aye, and she was a treasure trove of new experiences. He'd certainly never had such a deep conversation with a lass like this. 'Twas refreshing, and enjoyable all in itself. "If you are ever willing, mayhap you will allow me to give you pleasure."

Her eyes sparkled. "I thought Highlanders were all about maintaining a lady's honor."

"Your honor would never be in jeopardy with me." He brushed a kiss across her lips.

* * * *

"I'm sure it won't." What a revelation. There were many sides to Archie she'd had no idea existed. She liked. "May I kiss you?"

"You never have to ask."

Time for him to experience her twenty-first century way of taking charge. Grinning, she pulled the neckline of his shirt wider and exposed his glorious chest. Thank goodness she hadn't told him where she wanted to kiss him. She pressed her mouth to his flat nipple then teased the tight flesh. Ah-huh, she could get used to the Highlander's way of retribution.

"'Tis an interesting kiss." He caressed the sides of her breasts. "I wish equal rights to do the same."

"You've already—"

"Nay arguing." He rolled her onto her back, lifted her breasts clear of her shirt then laved the tips in the most erotic kiss. "So beautiful. My mouth waters for these sweet morsels."

"I'd say help yourself, but should we be doing this out here in public?" Even though surrounded by low bushes, anyone could walk around the corner.

"My chamber would be best for the way I wish to kiss you." He righted her shirt. "My apologies. You have a way of making me lose track of my thoughts." He heaved to his feet and tugged her up. "Let's return to the others."

"Good idea." There was no need for them to take things quite so fast. They wandered back to the village. His men had returned to work, and several labored on each wall. They molded clay into large bricks, and with a touch of water, smoothed out the surface. Others shaved the bark from a half dozen cut logs, preparing them for the high roof beams. "They work together so well."

"We're one clan. Do the fae no' labor equally as so?"

"I'd say they're too busy playing, or that's how it appears to me." Beside the fire, Mary was bent over a pot, rubbing her lower back. "I need to go and help her."

He gripped her hand. "I'd rather you take Mary home so she can rest. She tires easily this near her bairn's birth. James will aid you."

"It's still early. Will she go?"

"Night falls quick this close to winter, and 'twill be upon us within a few hours. She'll go."

James whistled as he worked, his arms coated to his elbows with the clay. "He loves it here."

"Aye, this is his clan, and one day he'll be chief. Mary finds great comfort in having him close while his father isnae here. He'll understand why he must return with you." He called out to James, "I need you to travel with your mother."

"Coming, Captain." James dashed to the water barrel, dipped his arms and scrubbed them clean.

This was what she'd missed in life, having family like this. A clan. She squeezed Archie's hand. "Stay out of trouble while I'm gone, okay?"

"I'm never in trouble, and I will see you this eve so we may continue our earlier discussion." He dropped a soft kiss on her lips then crossed to George and clapped him on the back. "Take our ladies home."

"Aye, Captain." George sauntered to the barrel, cleaned up and ruffled James's gloriously bright red-gold locks.

Hmm, provided they indulged in more kisses, that discussion could get mighty interesting. She hiked down the hill toward Mary, George and James on her heel.

Mary groaned and rolled her eyes as they approached. "I should complain. Three against one isnae fair."

"As you wish, my lady, but home you go." George offered her his arm, which she grudgingly took, then he pressed his other toward Marie.

"Thank you, George." Together they wandered across to the cart and she seated herself next to Mary on the front bench.

The driver slapped the horses' reins, and their guardsmen rode into their positions. They were off, following the trail beside the coast toward the forest. James bumped about on the bare raggedy boards behind, his feet swinging over the tail edge. The birds chirped and James added his own pretty trill.

"He's so content." She nudged Mary's arm. "You've raised a wonderful son."

"There's naught James loves more than being around his clan, although he is ready and longs for his training. I dinnae want to see him go, but 'tis past time he's fostered."

"Where will he go?" Fostering seemed like such a sad thing to do, to lose one's child when they needed you the most.

"To his Uncle Donald on Skye, provided the king has released the Chief of Sleat."

"Hold." George flung up a hand and the driver hauled the cart to a rumbling stop. "I'll scout ahead. Listen for my call." He galloped away and the warriors accompanying them inched their mounts closer. Such care was taken for their safety. She relaxed against the backboard. Even with the frustration she'd experienced today, there had been an equal number of new firsts.

Archie for one, and his kisses for—

"Did you hear that?" Mary peered into the trees then gripped the driver's arm.

"Nay, my—" An arrow thunked into his chest and he toppled from the bench.

Terrified, Marie screamed, and Mary's shrieks echoed in her ears.

"Down. We're under attack." A warrior bounded from his horse and covered them as an arrow shot whizzed by.

Another guardsman groaned then a blood-curdling battle cry pierced the air as a score of warriors crashed through the trees.

"Remain where you are," boomed a man from somewhere near the thick brush.

The guard protecting them launched to his feet then grunted. He hit the ground with a sickening thud, a massive battle-axe wedged into his back.

This couldn't be happening, had to be a nightmare.

She scrambled down and heaved the warrior onto his side. Blood flowed from his mouth, down his neck. His eyes were blank.

A dark shadow fell over her and the slain warrior. "Get. Up. Now. Or you shall be the next to die."

"Do as he says, Marie." Mary clambered down and grabbed her arm.

She staggered to her feet.

The murderer seized his axe and slung it into a catch at his side, splattering the dead warrior's blood.

"W-what are you doing here, Lachlan." Mary's grip tightened on her.

A thick buckskin vest covered Lachlan's dark tunic, and a strip of leather tied back his blond hair, the same pale shade as hers. "I've come to fetch you, sister. I hear Angus awaits his death in the king's dungeons. 'Tis time you returned to your clan."

"I go nowhere, and the king's men will come for you too."

He snorted. "No one comes for me and succeeds. Who is this lass?"

"Marie MacLean." Mary edged in front of her. "She's my kin, our kin."

"A MacLean?" He circled them both, inspecting her from head to toe. "Then why does she travel with MacDonalds?"

"She is fae. The Guardians of Dunyvaig sent her."

"Interesting." MacLean caught Marie's chin. "You bear a striking resemblance to my daughter, Bethag, though she is very young."

"I—I am a MacLean. My father was Locky." A shortened version of this man's name. "Please, don't hurt me." Katherine would be furious if she died.

"I would never take the life of one of my own clan, or the fae. You will live." He released her and signaled to his men. "Grab my nephew as well. We leave for the Rhinns and make haste. I wish to lure MacDonald into a battle. I want my land returned."

His men cheered.

This was not the kind of adventure she'd signed up for.

Chapter 5

With the skies toward Dunyvaig darkening, it appeared Archie's faerie had taken the sunshine with her. She'd been wrong to demand she go with him into battle when their women had to remain safe. He'd speak to her this eve and ensure she understood he needed her magic from a distance, not on the battlefield.

The pounding of hooves shook the ground as a rider galloped into the village. What was George doing back so soon?

"Attack." George slumped forward and spat out blood.

"What happened?" He caught George as he toppled.

"Mary. Marie. James. All taken." An arrow, embedded deep into his man's side, had him gasping for breath.

"Was it MacLean?" Fury taking hold of him, he wiped the blood from George's mouth.

"I didnae see. Scouting. Hit. The others. Dead and injured."

Damn it. He shouldn't have underestimated MacLean, not after he'd attacked so close to Dunyvaig. "I'll bring them home." He handed George into the care of one of the village women who'd tended the midday meal. He snatched his sword propped against the water barrel, holstered it across his back and hoisted himself onto George's destrier. Mounted along with his warriors, he raised an arm and pumped his fist into the air. "I want MacLean's head. Now."

A thundering roar boomed around him.

They would fight. To the death.

MacLean would not survive this attack.

* * * *

Anger thrummed fiercely though Marie. MacLean had killed or maimed their entire guard. He couldn't be allowed to get away with this.

"Pick up your pace, lass." A scraggly bearded guard prodded her from behind, his grass-stained tunic tattered and smeared with blood.

Arms bound behind her, she stumbled across the thick roots poking from the ground. Mary and James had been trussed as she had, and they walked together with MacLean's warriors surrounding them.

"What will MacLean do once we reach the Rhinns?" she whispered to Mary.

"Use us as bait." Shoulder lifted, Mary wiped her sweat soaked brow against her puffy blue woolen sleeve. "I cannae believe the lengths my brother goes to. He'll pay with his life for what he's now done."

"Archie will come, won't he?"

"He'll come, and he'll be after my brother's head." She drilled a stare into MacLean's back as he led them through the ever-thickening forest.

"This is bad, isn't it?"

"He'll have more men there, otherwise he would have made for the coast. Duart Castle on Mull is his stronghold, but he has homes on neighboring Jura and Coll. Archie will come. He'll no' fail us."

She shuddered, recalling exactly how intent Archie had already been after the attack on the village. His thirst for MacLean's death drove him, and now, she truly didn't blame him. Even she would be happy to see MacLean fall with how ruthlessly he'd killed. No. Slaughtered. So barbaric.

This was such a mess, and MacLean couldn't die. The king's men had taken Angus and Donald MacDonald. MacLean was the loose end to the blood feud, and she had to ensure his capture.

Goodness, how did she manage to get herself into these kinds of predicaments?

Some faerie magic truly wouldn't go amiss.

Mary panted as she slogged, each breath a struggle. And what kind of man made a heavily pregnant woman hike through such demanding terrain? So much for her ensuring Mary rested. At least James remained strong. He'd stayed close to his mother's side, encouraging her whenever she'd faltered.

MacLean had pushed them on throughout the long night, not taking a break.

It should have been a relief when dawn finally broke, but she had no idea how much farther they had to travel. Birds twittered, although one's trill seemed slightly off compared to the others.

"Halt." MacLean lifted a hand then responded to the bird's call with an identical answering of chirps.

Mary took a deep whiff. "There's a touch of salt in the air, and with the distance we've tread, we should be close to Loch Indaal."

Loch Indaal cut into Islay's southern end. She and Katherine had driven around the coastline, passing the sparkling waters of the loch from the ferry terminal the first day they'd arrived.

A man slid between the trees toward MacLean, his beady brown eyes surveying all as he came in alongside the chief. "My laird, there's no sign of any of the MacDonald galleys at sea."

"Yet," MacLean grunted. "Angus's second will come once he hears of my attack. Archie MacDonald willnae allow the capture of his kin to pass. We must continue on to our men who wait, drawing MacDonald toward Loch Gruinart where I wish to make a stand, on the land which is mine." MacLean scowled at Mary then strode toward her, flattening the underbrush as he did. Feet planted wide, he examined her. "How do you fare, sister?"

She turned her back and pressed out her bound hands. "Untie me. Unless you're scared I can best a man like yourself."

"I fear naught, but aye, I'll no' forget you besting me at sticks as a bairn. Your small hands aided you in the game. I could never halt the sticks from toppling." He loosened her knots, turned her around then rubbed her hands between his. "You still have an insolent mouth."

"I might, but I imagine it rivals your own."

"Aye, and you're as feisty as ever. Good. That will see you through." MacLean eyed the warrior closest to them. "They'll no' escape. Unbind the lad and lady too." His gaze slid away from Mary and over Marie. "So, we have one of the fae in our midst. Tell me of the little folk."

"They're rather annoying." Really annoying. His guardsman removed her rope, and blood pulsed down her arms and stung her fingertips. She shook her hands.

Mary stepped in front of her, moving eye to eye again with MacLean. "Marie was delivered to us after Archie made a wish. 'Twas a shock to discover she was a MacLean, but 'tis what happened."

"Yet she appeared from the circle of stones, nay surprise at all." He crossed his thickly muscled arms. "Which proves Dunyvaig Castle belongs to the MacLeans since a MacLean came forth from the guardians' circle."

"Aye, but she is of both clans, her mother a MacDonald." Mary gripped his arm. "You forget so quickly, brother. 'Twas you who agreed to my marriage with Angus. Why cannae you put your differences aside? Why cannae you return to Duart Castle and worry about the lands you already hold instead of fighting for those you do no'?"

"I fight, because eleven years ago the king and council commanded Angus and I settle our dispute by your marriage to him. You were forced to wed MacDonald, to patch a feud which has never been resolved, no' in all this time. Father gambled MacLean lands away, but I will fight until I get them back."

"You battle for the wrong reasons. You stole James from me when he was but five, and now you think to steal us both. There's been so much bloodshed and loss of life, on both sides. You will lose it all if the king states it so."

"The king willnae take my land from me. He can send as many summonses as he likes, demanding I present myself at Edinburgh, but I willnae bow to him, no' after I lost my sister to his so-called 'settling of the last dispute.'" He slammed a hand against his thigh. "Tell me how Angus was taken."

"He went to visit Donald MacDonald on Skye. They were both captured there, when they least expected it." Mary didn't quail, but told him straight.

"I see, then I should anticipate a visit from the king's men myself."

"They will come for you, mark my words." She thrust her chin toward him. Mary had guts.

"Aye, but mayhap to Mull, Coll or Jura. They willnae think to search for me here." He frowned then gently set his palm against her cheek. "I'm weary of fighting with you. I will return you home to your kin. 'Tis why I came for you. I should never have let you wed a MacDonald."

"You've just taken me from my kin. You cannae defend your actions and spout your need to return me into the MacLean fold as your reasoning why. I know the truth, and willnae be swayed." Tears leaked from Mary's eyes. "I hate and despise you, Lachlan."

"Aye, little sister, as much as you love me. I've no doubt of it."

"Islay is my home. James is heir to Dunyvaig, and I cannae leave my bairns behind."

"I'll rescue your young ones in time."

"They dinnae need rescuing. You've brought James and I right into the middle of your fight again. Dinnae you see what you've done? Archie willnae rest until James and I are back where we belong." She sent a pleading look at Marie. "Nor his faerie. You must see reason."

"I've always seen reason." His gaze darkened to the deepest shade of midnight-blue. "And Islay will be returned to me."

"So you wish to steal your nephew's heritage?"

"Nay, I wish to see it placed in my son's hands, as Father should have placed the Rhinns in mine. Hector is my heir and will be the fifteenth Chief of MacLean. My line shall rule Islay, no' Angus's." Snarling, he leaned in. "Make no mistake, sister, I will see this done."

"I hate you, Uncle." James burst through and plowed into MacLean, hands smashed against the massive chief's chest. "I hate you, just as Mother hates you."

"James, nay." Mary tried to pull him back.

MacLean snickered, grasped the boy and shoved him away. "Calm down, James. I only wish to see to your mother's welfare."

"I hate you. I hate you." Cheeks puffed, James's face flared red.

"Leave my son alone, Lachlan. You've hurt him enough."

"Your son will be a man afore you know it, and a little pain willnae go amiss in strengthening him."

Mary clutched James to her, holding onto him like a lifeline. She glared at MacLean. "Leave us be. Just leave us be."

"You'll come to understand what I've done, in time." He stormed toward the front of his men. "To Loch Gruinart," he bellowed. "Let MacDonald come for us, but we fight for Islay."

A cheer went up and Marie wrapped her arms around Mary

and James. "I'm so sorry this has happened to you both."

"'Tis no' your fault. Listen, both of you," Mary whispered madly in their ears. "At the first sign of opportunity we escape, together. I willnae allow Lachlan to use us against our own clan."

"Aye, Mother." James nodded, his eyes narrowed. The lad would soon become a man, his childhood, though, already gone. "Say aye, Marie."

"Yes." She kissed his forehead. "Together. I promise we'll escape together."

It was the easiest promise to give. Now to see it through.

* * * *

Archie tightened the birlinn's ropes as he and his men sailed along the coast of Loch Indaal. Last eve he'd ridden with his men as far as he could through the forest then gone on foot. MacLean's tracks had led west. The Rhinns. MacLean was making a stand, and having taken Marie, Mary and James, it was a devious one.

Half his men trailed MacLean to keep an eye on his movements while he'd returned to Dunyvaig and gathered more men. This war couldn't be fought without his best warriors at hand.

Soon after, he'd set sail.

John captained another birlinn, their MacDonald flag raised high on both vessels as they'd searched the coastline.

MacLean wished a fight, and he had one.

Marie consumed his thoughts. He never should have allowed her out of his sight. She was his to protect, and if something happened to her because of his failing, he'd never forgive himself.

"Captain. Will stands in wait."

On the edge of the forest the warrior in charge of the band on land, signaled to them. "To land, with speed," Archie ordered.

They crested the incoming waves, close to shore. He heaved

himself into the waist-high water. Surging through it, he slogged toward Will as his man jogged down the beach to meet him.

John too bounded from his galley and worked his way across. They met together where the waves pounded in and rolled up onto the sand.

"What news do you bring, Will?" It had better damn well be good.

"MacLean has no' been hard to track, Captain. 'Tis clear he wishes to leave a trail toward the Rhinns."

"What of the women and James?"

"Mary does no' appear as if she can walk much farther. Your faerie is aiding her as she can. I snuck as close as I dared for a look."

Which meant he could delay no more. He faced John. "I'll anchor here, take my men and come in on his rear. You sail ahead to Loch Gruinart and wait for me to join you with my additional numbers." He signaled to his warriors to disembark.

"I'll await your arrival." John gripped both Archie's forearms. "MacLean is prepared and this has been a tactical attack. He'll have more men awaiting him at the Rhinns."

"Aye, he will. He's making his stand, but then so are we." He returned John's strong forearm hold. "Per mare per terras, by sea and by land."

"We fight." John pulled him in then clapped his back. "Take care, brother. I'll see you at Loch Gruinart."

"Dinnae advance until I arrive." He'd fight by his brother's side. Together they'd hold Islay for their clan. He checked his holstered claymore then jogged across the beach and through the gap in the tree line. His men followed soundlessly in his tracks. A hundred yards in, he picked up the trail and motioned for them to fan out along his flank.

Stealthily, he tracked until he caught movement ahead. Eric and his other men closed in around him.

"How close are we?" he asked Eric in a hush. His best

tracker was a massive man, yet had the uncanny ability of slipping in and out of the smallest spaces.

"They rested for a mite of time then continued on."

Not a long enough rest for Mary's sake. What was MacLean thinking to take a woman so close to her time? His drive to kill MacLean strengthened. At least his numbers were strong, no matter the disadvantage he faced with the abduction of his kin. He'd have to rescue the women and James first, removing them from the possibility of harm. And preferably before MacLean reached the Rhinns. He couldn't have them becoming a target during the oncoming battle. "We head out. 'Tis time MacLean met his match."

Justice would be sought.

His mind was set.

Chapter 6

The scent of the sea disappeared as Marie trekked through the thick undergrowth. MacLean's marauding party had taken a fork in the path and veered away from Loch Indaal. Not a good sign. Loch Gruinart now lay directly ahead, perhaps five to seven miles, no more. If they were to escape, they needed to do something soon, and before they arrived at MacLean's camp and joined the remainder of his fighting force.

"Halt," MacLean called out, one hand raised as he stopped in a small clearing. He motioned two of his men forward then left with one of them to scout ahead.

She gripped Mary's clammy fingers. "How are you doing?"

"I need to tend to my needs." Gruffly stated as she shot a daggered look at the warrior guarding them. He should wash his face. There was sticky brown stuff on the pointy end of his whiskered goatee. Smelly too, like meat juice, likely from whatever he'd last eaten. "If we're simply standing here for a while, then it should be safe enough for us to take a moment," Mary snapped at him.

The warrior scrubbed his hand over the deep scar cutting across his cheek. "Once the chief returns ye can ask him."

"I cannae hold on any longer." Mary jabbed a finger into

his buckskin-covered chest. "You try carrying a babe and having the mite kick a storm on your—" She threw her hands into the air. "Oh, why am I trying to explain this to you. Those bushes will afford me the privacy I need. Marie, a hand if you please."

"Coming." She followed as Mary toddled around the brushwood.

"James," Mary called. "See to your needs as well. The trees yonder will be fine."

"Hold. 'Tis I who is in charge." The warrior grabbed James by the collar then addressed one of the other men. "Take the boy while I watch the women."

"You'll no' be watching us." Mary's lips pinched together as she snarled. "Unless you're afraid a woman in full bloom could possibly outrun you and all these men."

He growled under his breath. "You've a sharp tongue, my lady. A few minutes. No farther than those bushes."

"Aye, a lady. And dinnae you forget it." Mary snorted as she led Marie around the copse then hunkered down. "I spied Eric," she whispered wildly.

"You did?" She clutched her chest, her heartbeat a loud hammer in her ears. "The trees are so thick. Where? What do we do?"

"We wait and—" She glanced in the direction James had been taken. "Did you hear that?"

"No, hear what?"

A man slithered through the underbrush toward them, a dirk dripping with blood in one hand and a determined grimace on his face. Archie had come for them. He must have nerves of steel to do so while so many MacLeans surrounded them.

"Lass, dinnae look so surprised." He kissed her, hot and hard, and not nearly long enough. "I said you were no' to go into battle."

"I didn't have a choice."

"You do now." He tipped his head toward Mary. "Eric has

James. Stay as low as possible and follow my path. I have to get you two out of here afore I can give the signal for the others to attack. We'll weaken their numbers here, and you must be away so I can."

"Lachlan isnae here, and he has more men waiting at Gruinart."

"John already sails ahead. I'll deal with MacLean. You must go."

Mary nodded, hoisted her skirts over her knees then crawled as fast as she could away.

"Your turn." Archie nudged her to follow.

"You can't kill MacLean. Please. I know you don't believe I'm from the future, but I am." Goodness, he had the most beautiful molten gold eyes and they were focused solely on her. "You have to be careful too, or I won't be happy."

"You're here to aid me in my war against MacLean, not partake in it. His death is imminent, a mere matter of time." Those stunning eyes narrowed.

How would she get him to believe her? She was running out of time. "I won't leave you until you give me your word he won't die."

"Nay. You'll go as I command. I need you away from here. Now."

"Are ye ladies finished?" The warrior was close, and no, she wasn't even halfway done. As it was, there were far too many hotheaded men in this clearing. Any upcoming battle would be brutal.

"Go, or you risk bringing danger down upon Mary and James's heads by your actions. Do you wish that?"

"No." Damn it. And Mary had stopped to wait for her. She couldn't endanger her or James. Whipping back, she faced Archie. "You don't fight fair, and we will have a stern word about this the moment you get done here. An argument I'm going to win. You got that?"

"Aye, lass. I look forward to battling with you." He tipped her onto her belly then raised his dirk. "Stay low, and dinnae make a sound as you go."

"Don't kill MacLean. If you do, I'll be really angry." She scuttled after Mary. Angry, and perhaps even dead.

She crawled, trying hard not to slap her hands down. Yuck, was that blood? A trail led to a body half stuffed underneath the brush at the side. It was the warrior who'd guarded James, his eyes now glassy with death. A chill raced down her spine. Oh, what she wouldn't give to be back home and strolling her Gold Coast beach. She'd be guaranteed no death and disaster awaited her there.

No. She could do this. She had to keep moving.

"Marie, this way," Mary whispered as she motioned her forward. "Dinnae look, only move."

She met Mary's firm gaze and found the remainder of her strength. She kept crawling until a warrior with thickly furred boots stepped out from behind a tree and scooped Mary into his arms. It was Will. Mary was safe.

As she made the same tree, another warrior drew her to her feet. Eric. What a sight to behold. She clutched his shirt and swayed into him. "Eric, I love you."

"Thank you, lass, but dinnae tell the captain, or I shall be in more trouble than it's worth." His bushy red eyebrows fringed determined blue eyes. "You're safe now, as are Mary and James."

"Yes, but I left Archie alone."

"Dinnae worry about—"

A fierce battle cry rang out. Archie had been discovered.

"Hold tight, lass. The captain needs to be assured of your safety. You can no' be here." He slung her over his shoulder and her belly thumped into his rock hard shoulder as he raced them away. She clutched his pumping arms and tried to search for Archie. The trees were too thick.

Archie had to survive this battle. He couldn't fight the sheer number of MacLean's men in that clearing on his own.

The ground blurred, made worse by the speed Eric moved as the trees whizzed by.

"I smell the sea," James cried out as he sprinted alongside them.

"We're almost there, lad." The warrior cleared the tree line then halted on the beach. He lowered her to her feet.

Everything spun and she squeezed her eyes shut then shoved them open again. The stunning blue-green waters of the loch glistened. Freedom. And Archie's birlinn anchored offshore. She would rejoice, except— "Mary." She spun around.

"Here." Mary wriggled out of Will's arms then grabbed James. "We're all safe."

"I left Archie alone." Marie stumbled across and hugged the two of them. "How could I have done that?"

"Our men were close." Mary patted her back. "Dinnae fret."

"I still left him." Tears misted her eyes and trickled down her cheeks. When had Archie come to mean this much to her? Her heart squeezed tight. "I shouldn't have left him, no matter what he said."

"Nay. He'll be able to fight without fear now we're all away."

"He'd better." He damn well better.

The battle raged so close, yet too far away.

"Be safe, Archie. Come back to me." She sent her wish flying free.

* * * *

Archie lifted his sword high and blocked the warrior's swift blow. Their claymores clashed dead center, steel ringing loud against steel. With a roar, his warriors tore free from where they'd hid and met MacLean's men as they attacked.

The warrior Archie fought bellowed to another and his kinsman jumped the low brush and came in on his other side.

Two against one. This would be interesting.

"What have we here?" The second attacker twirled his blade. "Archie MacDonald, the MacDonald chief's second. This is a boon."

"Where's MacLean?" Archie rocked on his heels.

"Ahead, although ye can be assured he'll be disappointed he missed this."

The two men advanced from opposite sides.

The first warrior mouthed to his kinsman, "Three, two, one."

Their blades descended.

Archie spun his sword high and blocked both well-timed blows with one swing. He dropped low, kicked the first warrior off balance then swept his other leg out and kicked the second man.

They both fell forward, their blades sliding down each other's and impaling their chests. Blood gurgled from their mouths as they fell into a heap on the ground.

In the heart of the clearing, the battle raged. He had almost two warriors to one of MacLean's, but 'twas the man himself he wanted. MacLean should have heard the battle and returned by now.

"MacDonald."

He spun around, and a MacLean warrior struck his ribs with his blade. Pain ricocheted through him as he staggered back from the brutal sword blow. Hell. He should have been paying attention to the fight and not MacLean. 'Twas lucky he'd caught the flat of the man's weapon. No blood spilled.

"You killed two of my kin." The warrior raised his claymore. "You'll die for it."

"They killed each other, and you'll die for taking my kin." He circled the warrior. They matched each other in height and breadth, although that was no equal standing for the battle lust storming through his body. This was his land, his clan, and they'd taken his faerie. Archie landed several hard blows, then with one powerful strike of his claymore, knocked the man's sword away.

The warrior grabbed his dirk and aimed between Archie's eyes.

Archie swung his blade across the warrior's throat and ducked the dagger as it flew.

The warrior's eyes rolled as he toppled to the ground, his hands twitching as death took him.

Alert this time, he whirled, searching for MacLean among the warriors. No MacLean. Where the hell was their leader?

More than a half a dozen bodies littered the forest floor, thankfully none of his men. The odds were in their—

An ear-piercing whistle shrilled then Maclean's men turned tail and ran. Nay. He wasn't done with them.

"Captain." Gregor bounded across to him. "Do we give chase?"

Marie, Mary and James would be safe, but there was no certainty unless he had them secured behind Dunyvaig's walls. They came first.

"John awaits us at Loch Gruinart and with MacLean unaccounted for, we'll take the battle there." He pumped his fist in the air, shouting to his men, "We've won this fight and we will win the next."

A roar went up.

Aye, he would fight MacLean soon, and face to face. For now though, he wiped his sword across the grass then holstered it.

"To Loch Indaal!" He stormed down the trail and through the forest, his men pounding after him until he burst onto the beach.

Marie stood at the edge of the surf, her white-blond hair a tangled mess and her beautiful blue eyes fastened on him.

The tightness in his chest eased.

"Archie." She ran toward him.

He opened his arms and caught her, barely planting one foot back in time to stop them both from tumbling to the sand. "Lass, you seem rather eager to see me."

"Are you hurt?" Her hands darted all over his body. "There's a spray of blood."

"'Tis no' mine, although my ribs took a beating. 'Twas the luck of the fae I had with me." He snared her face between his hands and brought her gaze back to his. "What of you?"

"I'm fine. Mary's fine and so is James. They didn't hurt us. Let me see this beating." She clawed his shirt up and gasped. "That looks bad."

"'Tis naught but a bruise. It'll heal."

She tentatively touched the spot then glared toward the forest. "Who did this to you?"

"One of MacLean's warriors caught me off guard. It willnae happen again." Aye, resilient and feisty. She was all he'd ever dreamed of in a woman.

"It better not happen again. We're going to have a talk about this too. What of MacLean?"

"He never returned and once it appeared they would lose, they retreated." He stroked her cheek as longing to hold her rushed through him. "From now on, you dinnae leave my sight."

"That works for me, and I'm going to make sure you don't forget what you just said." She lifted onto her toes and inspected a scratch on his chin then another along his jaw. "You need to take more care. I couldn't stand leaving you the way I did."

"I would no' have been able to focus had you been there." Hell, the danger she'd been in this past day had driven him to the edge. He'd had to get her back.

"What do we do now?"

"We return to Dunyvaig. Mary and James are my responsibility, and I must ensure they are kept safe." He tugged her toward the birlinn.

Mary and James were onboard, as well of most of his men. A few still took dips in the water before climbing aboard. The salt was good for the wounds, and the water cleansed away the overpowering stench of blood.

At waist-depth, he turned Marie by the shoulders and looked into her eyes. "Would you care to take a dip?"

"Absolutely." She plucked at her shirt. "I'm sorry about the stains on this. You'll probably never loan me clothing again."

"I'll loan you a tunic whenever you wish. Hold on and dinnae let go." He wrapped her hands around his neck then pushed her backward. Down they went, his mouth covering hers as the water closed over their heads. He kissed her, sharing his breath until he had no more to give. Not yet ready to let her go but having no other choice, he hauled her to the surface.

"Oh." She shivered then twined her fingers into his hair. "You make taking a dip fun. I'm not going to argue if you ever want to do that again."

"Let's get you warmed up. There are plenty of blankets onboard." He led her to the birlinn and gave her a boost.

She clambered over the side, wrung out the ends of her shirt and tottered to the seat at the stern.

From under his area near the rudder, he nabbed one of his tartans and bundled her in it. Her cheeks were pink and her eyes sparkled, although she must be tired. Facing his men, he ordered, "Hoist the sail and set course for Dunyvaig."

Once they'd seen to his bidding and were well on route, he eased in beside her.

"Do you want to share this?" Marie unraveled one side of her blanket.

"Nay, the wind will dry me quickly. I want you to rest." He tucked the tartan back around her, tipped her legs onto the bench and settled her head in his lap.

"I'm not really tired."

"Aye, you are. 'Tis the rush of war that keeps you awake.

It'll calm when you do." He tucked her drying hair behind her ear. "Sleep. Now. That's an order."

"You can't order someone to"—yawning, she patted her mouth—"sleep."

"Orders are what I know best."

"So I've seen." She curled a hand around his thigh and snuggled. "Although if I fall asleep it's not because you ordered it, but because I want to be wide awake for later."

"For what reason, lass?"

Her eyelids drooped as she murmured, "To seduce you. I know what kind of man you are, and I want more."

Every muscle in his body tensed. "You've already done so."

"Oh, I haven't even begun to seduce you yet." She stroked the soft leather of his trews. Her breathing evened out, and slowly, she drifted off.

He relaxed.

She was safe, and close.

Exactly as he needed her to be.

* * * *

The boat rocked and dipped. Waves slapped against the birlinn's sides, the sound pulling Marie further toward wakefulness.

"Go back to sleep." Archie's voice floated over her then his lips brushed her cheek. "Sleep."

She stretched, wriggled onto her back and pushed her eyes open. Night had fallen, and the moon, hidden behind a layer of darkened cloud, cast Archie's face in shadow. "Where are we?"

"We're almost home."

"Oh, good." She cupped his stubbly jaw. "Thank you for coming for me. I'm not sure I actually told you that during my angry spiel."

"'Twas my duty. I gave you my promise of protection and I willnae fail you again."

"I know, but—" Using her elbows, she edged up and kissed

his chin. The man took everyone's protection right to heart. A soft heart indeed. "I realized something out there. I had no doubt you'd come. Your fighting nature was rather appealing at that point."

"You find me desirable?"

"I find you completely distracting, and I like it."

He frowned. "I too find you distracting, and at a time when I must concentrate on the battle ahead. I cannae allow you to become a part of it."

"You're too late. I already am." She kissed him again, this time on his bottom lip. "Let's distract each other. How soon until we're in your chamber and all alone? I have a terrible need to distract every inch of you."

"Careful." His cock hardened and poked into her lower back. "We're no' alone yet."

"Well, look at that." She snuggled against him and he growled under his breath. "I'd love to distract that part of you."

"As I would you, but no' here, even though 'tis dark." He slid her onto the seat beside him.

This warrior had no idea how independent twenty-first century women could be. Maybe there was a little bit of mischievous fae in her after all.

She was about to have some spirited fun.

Chapter 7

Archie wanted naught more than to carry Marie straight to his chamber, toss her onto his bed, see to her every pleasure then keep her locked safe behind Dunyvaig's walls. Damn his wish. He'd had no intention of bringing her this deeply into his battle.

"What's wrong? You look worried again, not that you've really stopped."

"The men require a short rest. At dawn, we'll sail to Loch Gruinart. John awaits me there." He stood as they rounded the tip into Lagavulin Bay. The faerie circle's stones, dimly lit by the torchlight near the entrance, called a silent welcome. "Lower the sail, all to oars."

"You know I have to come with you, right?" She rose and gripped his hand. "That's how my magic works."

"So you say, lass, but I dinnae wish to endanger you again." He called to Eric and Will, "Take us in."

His men bounded over the side of the birlinn, seized the bow and guided it toward the stone landing where the water lapped its sides.

A call rang out from his guardsmen atop the battlements. An answering shout of victory boomed from his men aboard.

"Archie?" Marie's gaze pleaded with him. "I meant what I

said about that's how my magic works. I can't aid you unless I'm with you."

"I need to see to Mary first. She can be even more obstinate than you. Must be in your dual clan blood." He sprang onto the stone steps then turned and aided Mary onto the landing. Holding her arm so she didn't slip, he led her along the grassy area of the lower courtyard and up the embankment to the entrance.

Mary glanced at him. "I know what you're going to say, but—"

"You're no' permitted to leave Dunyvaig until I've seen to MacLean, no' one step outside this keep."

"Please, Archie." Her riot of red-gold curls swayed around her waist as she shook her head. "I need to be able to return to the village."

"Angus will slit my throat if he hears I've placed your life in any further danger. Do you wish for me to have an early death?"

"Nay." Her shoulders sagged. "Must I truly remain here? Lachlan forges onward toward the Rhinns. I'm safe enough."

"MacLean took you once, and he may well try again. Here you will stay." He kissed her forehead then handed her into the care of her maid who bustled forward.

"Archie."

He swung around.

Marie hurried along the trail then halted beside the faerie circle. The look of longing on her face had him racing toward her. He pulled her away, steered her through the gates and beyond the temptation of the stones. "You must never enter the circle. 'Tis a sacred place. Do you understand?"

"Yes, I'll wait until your wish is done, but I'm coming to Loch Gruinart." She stopped in the center of the bailey. "You can't command me not to. We both know it's the right thing to do."

"You're under my care."

She took one step closer until the tips of her scuffed white boots touched his. "The last time we were separated, it didn't go well. I need to be where you are. I can't aid you with my magic otherwise."

"Captain." Will strode toward him. "The men have asked when you wish to set sail?"

"On the dawn's high tide. Ensure sufficient supplies are stocked for the coming days."

"Aye, Captain."

With a hand at Marie's back, he guided her inside and through the great hall. He called to one of the maids to bring a hot bath and a tray to his chamber. He led her up the winding stairs and into his room.

"We have to talk about this." Marie twirled around as he shut the door. "I'm not taking no for an answer."

Of course she wouldn't. Damn. Her resilience had its place, but not right now.

* * * *

Highlander men were far too obstinate for their own good. Well, this one had met his match, because so was Marie, and she wouldn't back down until he agreed. "I'm coming."

"I realize you wish to, but there must be another way." He bent before the hearth, lit the fire and stoked it into life.

At a knock on the door, he crossed then bid the two lads to enter. Barefoot and with sooty imprints on the knees of their loose-legged breeches, they heaved a tub before the fireplace then scurried out. A servant entered carrying a tray with two steaming bowls and a trencher of meat. She set it on the side table beside a basin and jug.

Another maid arrived next, set a drying cloth and bar of soap on the corner chair nearest the tub then laid an armful of clothing over the engraved lid of Archie's wooden trunk. A splash of deep red peeked through from underneath a fur cloak.

Enticed, she crossed the chamber and fingered the fine velvet gown. "Is this for me?"

"'Tis one of Mary's. She must have sent it." Archie closed the door behind the servants then held out a chair for her. "Come and eat."

"Yes, please. This looks amazing." She sat and breathed in the mouth-watering scent of mutton stew. Yum. A thick slice of bread was wedged half into it. She scooped it up, took a big bite then licked the richly flavored juices as they dribbled from the end. Delicious and hot.

"Is it good?" He knelt at her feet, tugged her boots off and set them before the fire to dry.

"The best I've ever tasted. Sit with me."

He pulled out a chair and sat with his knees brushing hers. With a spoon in hand, he ate. The maids returned along with the lads, each carrying a steaming pail of water, and once the tub was full, they left.

She almost cried at the glorious sight of the bath. Curling steam beckoned. "At home we have both hot and cold running water. It's piped straight into the bathroom where the tub sits. I don't believe I'll ever take the convenience for granted again."

"Would you like to bathe now?"

"Absolutely." She jumped up, slid her linen pants to the ground then reached for the hem of Archie's stained tunic. She owed him a shirt.

"Marie." Archie's voice cracked as he muttered her name. "What are you doing?"

"Getting in the bath. You did ask if I'd like to."

"No' afore me." He cocked a brow. "You dinnae wish to bathe alone?"

"Perhaps you missed the part where I spoke of seduction, so no, not if I can bathe with you. We'll relax together. You can handle that, can't you?"

He glanced from her to the tub. "I've never bathed with a

woman afore. Are you certain?"

"I'm after pleasure, which you said was on offer." She sidled against him. "Take this shirt off. I no longer need it."

"Aye, then it would be my pleasure." He hunkered down, skimmed his warm hands over her calves then slowly trailed them up as he rose. Heat raced along the path he touched, behind her knees and over her outer thighs. He lifted her shirt higher as he stroked upward. When he reached the lower curves of her bottom, he gazed into her eyes. "I feel naught covering you below. Where are your undergarments?"

"I'm wearing a thong. There's a small triangle of fabric at the front then it narrows to a thin piece of cotton that slides between my cheeks. Where I come from, women wear them."

His gaze burned a richer golden hue. "May I remove it?"

"I'm not sure why you haven't already." She turned around and wriggled her bottom. "Take it all off."

Hands clamped on her hips, he gripped the material of her shirt then lifted it over her head. She gasped as he puffed hotly against her bare skin.

"Magic," he moaned, caressing her bottom.

She leaned into him, against the hard length of his erection. "Yes, you wield a magic touch yourself. Feeling distracted at all?"

"I am far beyond that point." He played with the thin strip of cotton before tugging the thong down her legs. "Turn around, my faerie. I want to see the rest of you."

She almost slithered to the floor as she did. Such a need burned in his golden eyes as she fully faced him.

"So beautiful." His gaze consumed every inch of her. "I want to touch, and taste." He cupped her breasts, eased them together then licked one nipple. The raspy stroke of his tongue sent a bolt of pleasure to her core.

"I like how you touch me."

He grinned then swirled around the tip. "I like it far more."

"Then bring on the pleasure. I want my Highland warrior. I want you."

"Aye, and I shall deliver." He sucked her nipple deep into his mouth and her knees buckled. He swept her up then lowered her into the tub. The warm water cascaded over her skin, adding more heat to the fire racing through her blood.

"Come here." She clutched his shirtfront and tugged it free of his pants.

"Let me undress first, lass." He stripped off his shirt. Muscled shoulders, broad and strong, spoke of the hours he must practice with his sword. What a wickedly wide chest. His abs rippled, and that delicious tease of dark hair narrowing down his rigid belly disappeared into his pants.

"Take it all off." Gawking at him was a pleasure all unto itself. After the trialing time she'd had, being close to him, touching him, was all she desired. "I can't believe you're going to be mine."

"Aye, all yours." He kicked off his boots then shoved his dark pants down his thickly muscled legs and off. His cock sprang free and brushed his belly.

"Mmm, mine." She squirmed back to make room for him.

He stepped in and eased down, sloshing water over her chest. After nabbing the soap, he lathered it, his gaze smoldering as it remained on hers. "Lift your feet and place them against my chest."

She did, his crisp chest hair tickling her sensitive soles.

With the thick mound of bubbles, he massaged her heel, the high arch and around her toes. He did the same with her other foot, his thumbs kneading with delicious strokes. "Do your feet ache?"

"Yes, as do other parts of me. I'm not used to tramping through a forest for mile upon mile, but I like the payoff if this is it." She rested her head against the rim and her hair swirled around then settled over her breasts.

"Dinnae cover yourself." He flicked her hair away and tweaked her nipple.

A fiery tingle radiated from the sensitive tip.

"You like such touch?" He watched her every move.

"I like everything you've done so far. I think you're far better at seduction than me."

He stroked her calves then worked the muscles of her legs until her lower limbs wobbled.

Hands on her thighs, he dragged her closer, his legs underneath her body as he kept her afloat over him. "I've got you. Relax and enjoy."

"If I relax anymore, I'm going to be a puddle of nothing." She swept her hands underneath her bottom and grasped his powerful thighs. Blisss.

He eased his soapy hands over her ribcage and around her back then worked bubbles into her hair, his fingers firm on her scalp.

"You are so good at that too."

"I need to touch more of you." He caught her legs, lifted them over his shoulders and brought her right up against him.

Her mind raced in a hundred different directions as he skimmed the inside of her thigh. Bathing with him was so intimate. "Okay, but take it slow. I've not done this before."

"I'll keep you intact." Golden eyes twinkling, he brushed over her entrance. "I give you my word."

"I know you will." Even now, he thought of protecting her. He dipped his finger along her folds then rubbed her clit. Moaning, she squeezed her eyes shut. "Please, yes."

"Look at me, Marie. I want to see your desire and feel what you feel."

"I feel it all." She looked into his eyes as he plunged one finger deep inside. She bucked as he stroked, harder and faster, until he curled his finger into a spot that had her arching out of the water.

She wanted her Highlander to touch her, in every single way, as she wanted to touch him.

Her pulse skittered out of rhythm, and before she lost her mind, she skimmed the hard length of his cock. Big and strong. His shaft was made to send a woman to the heights of ecstasy. She pumped him in sync with how he stroked her, matching him caress for caress, eager for him to feel as she did.

He groaned, long and low, the sensual sound sending a thrill through her. Then he released her legs and with one arm around her waist lifted her against him. He took her mouth in a hot kiss as he returned to stroke deep inside her with his finger.

What a world of new sensation. Yet still she wanted more, to experience whatever he could give her in whatever time they had. "Faster, Archie."

"Hell, you're so tight." He increased his rhythm, his thumb rubbing her clit.

Oh, sooo good. She moved with him as her orgasm built.

"Come for me, lass."

"Not without you." She pumped him harder as she balanced on the edge of a precipice she wanted to fly from, but wanting him to take the jump right along with her.

"I'm there, my sweet."

He flicked her clit and she soared. Her core rippled with wave after wave of pure bliss, and a bright kaleidoscope of colors burst in a stunning display behind her eyelids.

He'd taken her over, from the inside out and she never wanted to leave the wonder of his embrace.

* * * *

As Marie came around his finger, Archie could no longer hold the sensations storming through his body back. Her sweet hand on his cock had delivered unaccountable pleasure, her responsive body even more so, and now with her release, he allowed himself his own and followed her over the careening edge of no return.

He shuddered in her hand, spurting his seed in one long stream. She was so beautiful, her face awash with delight. He only wished to see her like this, to revel in the moment as they came together.

"Archie," she murmured as she locked gazes with him. "I adore bathing with you, feeling your hands on me as I touch you."

"'Twas the most enjoyable bath I've ever had." He cradled the back of her head in his hand. "I wish for each one I take to be with you."

"You've already made your wish, although I love the interesting turn it's now taken." She clasped his face and dragged his mouth back to hers. She kissed him, sighing softly in his mouth.

Damn it. Her kiss was stirring his cock back to life. That had never happened so quickly before. He pulled away. "The water's getting chilly. I wish to take you to my bed."

"Now that's a wish you can have."

After rising to his feet, he seized the pail of clean water, held it over her head and let half sluice her body. He sloshed the remainder over himself then aided her out. He nabbed the cloth and patted her dry. So alluring, her creamy soft skin beckoned him for another touch.

"Thank you." She ran a finger in a saucy swirl down his chest then nudged him toward the bed. He fell onto it and she followed, smiling wickedly as she crawled up his legs. "Now, it's time for retribution."

"You're adapting well to the Highlander way."

"I'm learning from the best." She cupped his balls and heat shot to his cock, hardening him impossibly further. Then she dipped her head and licked him, one long teasing stroke from root to tip.

Oh hell, he would never be able to hold off if—

She settled her lips over his head then took him deep.

"Marie." He jerked as her sweet mouth seared him. She palmed his balls and caressed the top of his sac. 'Twas torture, unlike any he'd ever suffered on the battlefield. "Halt," he croaked.

She sucked harder and he rocked his hips, pushing deeper inside her mouth. He should stop her. He should pull out. A sexual haze consumed him and he barely found enough sense to drag her up his body. "Your pleasure comes first."

"Meany." She licked her lips as though thoroughly enjoying every second of his anguish.

"I wish to give you pleasure again, and I willnae come until I have." He tipped her onto her back, and every inch of her flesh was lit by the flickering flames. Where did he start? Her breasts were full, the tips hard. His mouth watered for a taste of those first. They were deliciously sweet, and he needed more. He stroked down the valley of her breasts to her belly. Lower still, shimmery white-gold curls shone. "I need to get my fill of you, Marie."

"Take what you wish." She clasped his face. "After you kiss me."

Blood pounding, he kissed her, and the temptation of her mouth consumed his thoughts. His faerie held a potent enchantment he couldn't resist. His wishes would continue to mount, and would soon outnumber any she could ever grant. He had no doubt.

"I feel hot." She rubbed her chest against his, her nipples, so incredibly hard, scraping across his flesh. "I never want to forget this night."

Neither did he.

The way she looked at him, with such longing and trust, would be forever seared into his mind and soul.

Sweeping over her ribcage, he wished to adore her lush breasts. They would be his. He fingered one tip while he licked the other. Nice and slow, so he could savor the taste.

Rising into his touch, she pressed her breasts harder against him. He wanted more. He teased his teeth over the sensitive tip, taking a second before drawing the bud deep inside his mouth. He sucked. Hard.

His efforts won him a soft cry, hardening his cock until it jabbed the inside of her thigh.

"You like that?" He released her breasts then rose and edged his lower body farther away from the enticement of her entrance. He had to take care.

"Yes, and where are you going?"

"To make my mark." He nuzzled her neck then drew the soft flesh into his mouth until her breaths came in short gasps.

"I've never been marked before."

"Then I shall give you more than one. I wish to see these marks in the morn and recall exactly how I gave them to you." He kissed across to the other side of her neck and worked on another, this one slightly larger since his control was slipping further away. Huh. Slipping? He had no control at all, his cock hammering at him to take her.

Never had his desire for a woman ridden him so hard.

"Archie." She twisted her head and seized a breath. "I'm going to come from your kisses alone."

"Aye, come as you please." He spread her folds and she pressed her mound into his palm. Beautiful. And with her breasts bobbing so close to his mouth, he couldn't deny returning to them and enjoying another sample.

Below, he stroked a finger through her heat then plunged in and rubbed the spot she'd adored before.

She gasped and bucked against him and his balls tightened, his cock twitching.

Hell, he might still come before her if he didn't see to her pleasure now. She was so slick and close, her soft cries encouraging him.

He pushed a second finger in and ground his cock into her

hip to halt his release. It didn't slow his need but accelerated it.

"Archie." She screamed his name as she thrashed underneath him. Her tight channel tightened around his fingers and locked him firmly in place.

She was almost there, and he was lost, his balls on fire as her inner muscles clamped down and dragged his fingers in.

"I'm right here with you," he growled as his seed rushed forth across his blankets.

He collapsed on top of her, his wee faerie draining him. Magic. She was a wonder he wouldn't be denied.

Chapter 8

As dawn neared, Archie stirred. Marie remained curled on her side, her bottom snug in the curve of his groin. A temptation, and almost beyond his endurance. Throughout the night, he'd loved her in every way, except the one that would be forever denied him.

He eased out of bed then halted as she stretched and blinked her eyes open. "Go back to sleep. You need your rest."

"It's dawn already?" She crawled toward him, her breasts swaying full and heavy as she did. "You're not leaving without me."

"My men await."

"Then I'll hurry." She scrambled off the bed and stood eye to eye. "I have to come. I can't aid you with my magic any other way."

"You should remain here."

"Nope. No can do." She crossed to his trunk, swiped the red gown from the top and drew it over her head. The velvet skimmed her hips and fell in a swish to her ankles. She laced the white ribbons, her beautiful breasts disappearing within the tight bodice. "Do I just tie a ribbon at the top?"

"Aye, allow me." He took over, securing it along the square neckline edged with white lace. "I cannae take you with me. 'Tis too dangerous."

"You also can't leave me behind. I thought we covered the part where it's best I remain within your sight." She caught his hands and kissed his palms. Her tender touch sent another resurgence of heat to his groin. "The safest place I can be is with you, and you did wish for this."

He detested his wish, yet if he hadn't made it, she wouldn't be here. She was safest with him. The fae wouldn't have sent her if he didn't have need. "I willnae have you near the heart of the battle. You'll remain at camp, or wherever I deem fit. You'll also follow my every order."

"Whatever you ask, I shall do." Her agreement was swift. Aye, she'd do as he bid.

"You'll have a guardsman assigned to you. Eric." He grabbed the fur-lined cloak, secured it around her shoulders then quickly dressed himself.

"Great. As long as I'm close to you, that's all that matters." She raced across to the fire, grabbed her leather boots and yanked them on. "Could I borrow a brush?"

"Next to the basin on the side table."

"Thanks." She worked the brush through her hair then ran it through his. "You won't regret taking me. I promise you."

"I'm sure I will." On his way to the door, he grabbed his plaid. He was out of choices, but regardless, he'd ensure his woman would remain clear of the fighting.

He'd make certain of it.

* * * *

Clutching her skirts, Marie hurried after Archie down the winding stairwell. Unused to wearing such cumbersome clothing, halfway down she missed a step and teetered on the edge.

In a flash, Archie was there, catching her around the waist. "Take my arm."

"Could I borrow a pair of pants from one of the lads? I

rarely wear dresses, and as beautiful as this one is, I might need another option." She negotiated each step with more care.

"I'll procure additional clothing afore we leave." He stepped into the great hall, led her outside and across the inner courtyard.

She breathed deep, allowing the crisp air scented with the sea's spray to fully awaken her. They passed under the arch and down the trail. The gently sloping hill leading to the bay was scattered with rocks, but from this vantage point, the view was stunning. She raised a hand to her brow, the gold from the sunrise almost blinding as it shimmered off the flat sheet of water. "I've never seen it so calm."

"The winds will rise. 'Tis never calm for long in the isles."

His warriors loaded provisions onto the birlinn. The men were more heavily armed today, carrying swords, battle-axes, and bows and arrows. Not unexpected. She curled her fingers more tightly into Archie's arm. "I can't believe you have to live this way."

"Is it no' so for the fae?"

"I have no idea." She frowned, hating he still believed her to be one of them. "My magic truly comes from my knowledge of this time, not the little folk. I'm not sure I'll ever convince you, but I'm going to keep trying." She traversed the landing.

"There is naught you can say to sway my mind." He lifted her into the boat without losing a step. "Wait here for me. I'll return shortly."

"Alrighty then, honey," she called out as he marched away. "The little lady will remain here." Men, they thought they ran everything.

He laughed as he jogged up the grassy rise.

Chuckles resounded from a few of his men as they took their positions at the oars.

"You lot better be laughing with me, and not at me. We fae are an antsy lot."

She eased down the center aisle, sat on the bench at the stern and fluffed her skirts around her. Katherine had always adored dressing up in long gowns as a child. She'd love this era. Her heart squeezed. She missed her sister and longed to see her, to hold her. This morning she'd not looked upon the faerie circle. She did now. Her amulet wasn't visible from this low down on the water, but the perimeter stones remained solid and strong. The circle was her way back, provided she could see to Archie's wish.

Back straight, she focused all her energy on thinking positively, or at least she did until Archie stepped out from the gates and strode toward her. He carried himself as a leader of men, his stride purposeful and his determination unwavering.

Oh, and what that man could do with his determination. She tingled anew, from her head to her toes. He'd devoted attention to every single inch of her during the night. Her Highlander from another time was a man she wanted more of, and for as long as she was here.

He bounded into the boat, a bundle of clothing tucked under his arm as he hiked toward her. His steps slowed as he gazed at her neck then with his lips lifting, he leaned in and kissed her, tantalizingly hot. "Stow these garments under the seat, and Marie, I want to as well."

She touched the sensitive spots on her neck. "You're very territorial."

"I simply want what is mine." He took his position at the rudder and bellowed, "Let's sail. John awaits us at Loch Gruinart."

The men plunged their oars in and heaved. With no wind, the sail remained down, forcing them to rely on manpower alone. It was mid-morning before they neared the southern tip of Islay and hit the cross breeze of the sound.

"Hoist the sail," Archie called. The wind caught it and it unfurled with a hearty slap. Two men heaved the ropes into their secured position and knotted them. "Hold onto something, Marie."

She gripped the bench as they shot off along the coastline. The crisp wind whipped her hair across her face and numbed her nose and lips. A nasty draft swept under her skirts and chilled her legs. Goodness, the weather could turn in an instant in the isles. She tucked her skirts under her as best she could. "What happens once we get there?"

"I'll find John and confer with him." He brushed his thumbs under her eyes. "You need more rest. I kept you awake too late."

"I'm not complaining. The night wasn't nearly long enough for me." She kissed his stubbly jaw. "I want another one, with you all to myself."

"As do I, lass, though first you shall rest."

"Rest is totally overrated." Grinning, she slid onto his lap, wrapped her arms around his neck and nuzzled into his silky brown hair. "Will it be possible?"

"Rest? Aye, provided you close your eyes."

"I meant another night, with you."

"For now you need to obey my orders."

"You like ordering me about far too much, but aye, Captain, I'll do as you bid." She snuggled against him and sighed. "Just this once."

* * * *

Archie's men scurried about deck. With an adjustment to the rudder where he sat on the rear bench seat, he maintained their course along the coastline. They worked together with ease, his men rarely requiring instruction. They were islanders and seafarers, the waterways of the Inner Hebrides their home.

Nestled against him, Marie dozed. How could he have agreed to bring her on such a mission? He'd been so determined before this morn to keep her safely within Dunyvaig's walls, and now, she slept as he traveled into battle.

He stroked her hair, longing to have her back in his bed

with her glorious golden mane floating over his pillow and their combined scents mixing as he devoured every inch of her body. Instead, he allowed her gentle breaths warming his chest to soothe the raging need inside him.

His cock hardened, and he wished for her to ease the ache as she had throughout the night. Hell, after their bath when she'd wrapped her lips around him, he'd almost come. More than once, he'd struggled to hold back from thrusting inside her, to having her sweet channel tighten around him as she'd done with his fingers. If only he could, and be assured his seed wouldn't take.

"Archie," she murmured. "You feel tense. What's going on?"

"Naught. I didnae mean to wake you."

She rubbed his chest then settled her palm over his heart. "Is it the coming battle?"

"Aye, but 'tis more." He leaned closer, his voice low. "I have wishes aplenty, to be buried deep inside your beautiful body."

"You do?" She sank her bottom into his groin, coming into direct contact with the steel pike in his trews. She smiled, her lips lifting so deliciously. "Do you remember when we talked about protection at the village?"

"I said I would protect you against all things. I explained my position."

"You did, but where I come from, women truly do care for themselves, ensuring we're protected as necessary. I can't get with child, or at least not for the next couple of months."

"Because of your clever magic?" He kissed her nose. "'Tis still too great of a risk."

"Well, it's not magic as such. I had a, hmm, let's just say I took precautions, and they're ninety-nine percent effective."

"What precautions do you speak of?" He frowned, not caring for her talk of the future again. She was fae, yet she continually argued she came from a time far from now.

She patted her arm. "Something I had done right here."

"And you believe your arm can protect you against what goes on far below? Lass, your notions are becoming more far-fetched by the day."

Smiling, she tapped his nose. "You should see what options are actually available for far below. In my time men can wear condoms, thin films of rubber that slide around your—" She rubbed against his groin with her bottom. "Well, that part of you right there. In fact, in the future, women rarely die from childbirth. We're medically more prepared. Do you truly not wish for a family of your own one day?"

"I've nay desire to take a wife and see her lose her life. What of you? Do you wish bairns?" The thought of her body ripe with another man's child had his gut clenching, in the worst possible way.

"I'd be lying if I said no. I'd like three or maybe four."

"Captain."

Eric motioned toward land. Damn, he'd been so engrossed with his faerie he'd sailed off course. The rocks loomed. He jerked the rudder and steered them back alongside the coast.

"That must have been a first." Marie laughed and he swatted her backside.

"Behave. You are far too distracting."

"Yes, but I thought we were in agreement for that. Captain, in case you missed it, you may distract me as often, and in as many ways as you'd like."

He should like very much.

Far too much.

* * * *

Marie's heart lightened as they sailed along the coast. Hours had passed and they now cruised up the western shoreline, the beach a thick ribbon of golden sand more similar to her homeland. The grassy moors rolled into the distance, awash with tiny white clover flowers.

"This is such a beautiful place." She squeezed Archie's arm. "I can see why you love this land so much. Is that Nave Island?"

"Aye, it sits opposite the entrance to Loch Gruinart. Gruinart is a thin stretch of water, nay more than a mile wide for the most part, but it runs four miles deep. There's little room for maneuvering once we enter. On the low tide, ships can become trapped by the sand bars. John will have made berth no' far from here to ensure that does no' occur."

A flock of birds took flight from the north and soared across the inlet to the south where thick rushes swayed in the brisk sea breeze. "Where will John have made camp?"

"The forest, farther inland. He'll be lying in wait for MacLean, or searching for him."

A mile in, they came across John's birlinn anchored in the shallows with two guards remaining onboard. Archie ordered the sail down and his men rowed until they made berth beside the other vessel.

She grabbed her clothes and followed him to the bow where his men bounded into the water. He too jumped. No wonder these men were so conditioned to the cold water since they were always in it. She firmed her resolve, scooted over the side.

Archie caught before she hit the surface. "Only one of us needs to get wet, my sweet." He juggled her higher against his chest and waded in.

"Well, I'm glad it's you. I'm sick of water squidging about in my boots. So, what's the plan? A nice long romp across land? I can't believe how much exercise I've had lately. People pay big-time for such things at their local gym back home."

"Nay, there shall be no romping for you."

"But we agreed we'd stay together."

"We shall, though once I'm assured of John's position and that I'm no' leading you into any danger." He deposited her gently on the sand. From the stockpile of weapons his men had laid out, he grabbed a wrist sheath and dagger. "Come with me."

"Captain, we need to have words." She was back to square one. With him, but not with him. Argh, how frustrating.

"Words arenae needed. That was an order, one you must obey." He tugged her over the sandy dunes then checked the area. "You're out of view. Change now while I keep an eye out."

"I need to speak to you about MacLean. I thought I'd have more time." She tossed the cloak, unlaced her gown and slid it down her body and off. The wind held such a bite, and as quick as she could, she yanked on the breeches and belted them. The tunic was too large, but she pulled it on then rolled the cuffs. "I've told you my magic comes in the form of knowledge. I don't want you to kill MacLean, just capture him. No killing. You got that, right?"

"You've a strange way of speaking, as if you're ordering me about. Nay, the only way to win this war is by MacLean's death." With his lips pinched together in a tight line, he nabbed her cloak, slung it over her shoulders then secured it. "Your life isnae tied to his. You're living here. Now. In this time. You cannae tell me otherwise."

"Archie." The man wouldn't listen. "I've not lied to you. I'm from the future. You have to consider my request."

"And I've told you 'tis impossible." He lifted her arm and slid the sheath he'd chosen around her wrist. After slotting the dagger in place, he muttered, "Keep this on. You must remain armed at all times."

"It won't matter how well armed I am. The only danger I'm in right now is from you." She caught his face between her hands and kissed him, one breathtakingly deep kiss he better not forget as he walked into battle. "Think about what I've said, and come back to me. No more scratches, and no killing."

His gaze darkened. "His death is imminent."

"Then so is mine." She snatched her gown from the ground and strode back over the dunes to the others. She certainly had her work cut out for her. It was no wonder the fae had sent her since any other woman probably would have gone insane by now.

"Eric," Archie snapped, hot on her heels. "You're to stay with Marie. Guard her well."

"Aye, Captain." The red-bearded warrior nodded then walked toward her.

She stood still as Eric stopped at her side. Archie was leaving, without even another backward glance. He marched to the front of his guard and signaled for them to head out.

They marched in a solid line until they became a mere dot in the distance. Gone. She jiggled from foot to foot, beyond anxious. They should have remained together. Well, she'd remedy that and insert her own orders.

"Come on." Eric gripped her elbow. "There's nay need to worry. We have a stronger, larger force than MacLean, and we know our own land better than he ever could."

"MacLean is sneaky."

"The captain's aware. Send him your faerie magic. 'Twill never go amiss."

If only she could wield true magic instead of her wits to sort this mess and get back to her sister. Mum had died before her time, but she and Katherine wouldn't. She was an independent woman, and she didn't need to rely on a man like Archie thought she did. She wouldn't let him kill MacLean.

Sure, she detested MacLean as well, and she certainly didn't care for her ancestor or his tyrannical ways, but she needed him to atone for his behavior as he should before the king, and for that, his capture was necessary. There was no other way.

Two men remained onboard John's birlinn. "Are we boarding Archie's birlinn or staying here on the beach?"

"Whichever you wish."

"The beach please." She had to come up with a plan to

sway Archie. He'd be mad if she followed him, but too bad. He'd left her no choice.

"Ah, Eric, I could really use a moment of privacy." She shoved her knees together and squished up her face, mimicking Katherine needing to use the convenience at her best. "I fear it's urgent."

His face reddened. "The captain said to guard you well. You cannae leave my sight."

"I don't believe he meant that well. I'll be on the other side of the dunes, not far away at all. Please. I've really got to go."

"A few minutes. Nay more." He shook his head as if detesting his agreement.

"Thanks." A few minutes would have to be enough. She tossed him her rolled dress and scurried away.

If she played this right, she could keep hidden behind the barrier of sand dunes for some distance. It would give her a good head start for sure, and right now, every minute counted.

Once out of his sight, she ran, the chilly wind streaming through her hair and flapping her cloak behind her like a cape.

MacLean wanted it all when he already had so much. Half of Jura, the Isles of Mull and Coll. Now he wanted Islay, or at least the west. Archie would never let him have an inch of this land. He would fight to keep it in Angus MacDonald's hands.

Only the king could settle this whole war. MacLean had received a summons and should have traveled to Edinburgh. These Highlanders were too damn stubborn for their own good.

She veered to the left and used the edge of the rushes to aid her in picking up speed. This was such a wild land, yet so—

A man rose out of the thick grasses and nabbed her around the waist. She lost her balance and careened head over foot, the man forced to fly with her. They landed, his gritty hand clamped over her mouth.

Fighting for a breath, she stared into the dark blue depths of Lachlan MacLean's eyes. Oh great. How on earth had he gotten here without detection? The man was a snake.

"You appear surprised to see me, Marie." His gaze drilled into her. "'Twas a shame MacDonald left so soon. At least I'm no' leaving empty handed though, no' now I have you." She tried to pry his fingers loose, but he tut-tutted. "I want this land on the west, and I wouldnae mind a touch of your faerie magic. How willing are you to join with your true kin? Give me your answer, but dinnae draw attention to us, or it shall be at the consequence of your death."

She nodded, and he lifted one finger. Mumbling, she answered, "Your death is the last thing I want."

"That's a good start." He removed another finger. "I'm a fair chief to my own clan."

History had stated he'd commanded the respect of his people. Historians paid tribute to his memory in the works she'd read, so he had to have some redeeming qualities. Perhaps she'd yet to witness them, not that she had a lot of choice. He held the cards.

"Give me your answer afore your guard comes searching for you."

"I'm willing. If you wish my magic, you shall have it."

Slowly he released her, heaved himself to his feet then offered her a hand. "We leave, now."

Three heavily armed warriors rose from their hidden spot within the dense rushes.

"Where are we going?"

"My men await at camp in the forest. We'll run." He gripped her hand tighter and they raced across the moors. Archie would be furious she'd left Eric, and his rage would know no bounds once he discovered she'd willingly gone with MacLean, well, willingly enough.

"Please forgive me, Archie," she whispered under her breath. "I can be a little impulsive at times."

Chapter 9

"I left you guarding Marie. What the hell are you doing here, Eric? And where is my woman?" Night had fallen and Archie scowled at his man within the small clearing where John and his men waited.

Eric scrubbed a hand over his face. "She's gone. No' long after you left she asked for privacy. I gave her a mite of time then went in search of her."

"Was she taken?" He wanted to grab Eric and shake him until his teeth rattled. How had he allowed her to leave his sight?

"Aye, but first she ran for some distance following your path. There were clear signs of a scuffle in the sand, then her tracks and those of several others led north."

"Are you saying MacLean has her?"

"Aye."

He stormed back and forth across the clearing, furious he'd once again let Marie down and allowed the enemy to take her. Still, she was strong, and she would know he'd come for her. Damn it. She must have been worried to have tried to follow him. He should've listened to her instead of brushing off her concerns. She wasn't from the future. Couldn't be. Nay, she couldn't be. But why was she so adamant she was? He stopped before Eric. "How far did you track her?"

"As close to MacLean's camp as I could. 'Tis three miles, mayhap a touch more. He holds a position high on a thickly concealed rise."

John cleared his throat from where he leaned against a wide tree trunk. "We discovered his camp this afternoon but were awaiting your arrival." He pushed off, crossed and seized his shoulder. "'Tis time to attack, brother. Our force is now complete."

"I willnae have Marie caught in the middle of this battle." It would kill him to see her harmed.

"We're out of options."

"I forced her to make this decision. She was captured because I didnae take enough care."

"You wish a rescue first?" John cocked a brow. "That will be near impossible now MacLean's joined with the rest of his men."

He needed to slit his own throat for allowing Marie to be captured again.

Grasping his brother in a firm forearm hold, he muttered, "Per mare per terras, by sea and by land. We fight."

"Go first if you wish and get as close to your woman as you can." John returned his hold, his grip firm. "I'll gather the rest of the men and be close behind. The time has come. We battle."

"Aye, MacLean will die this day, by my sword and no other's. He's taken what's mine, and he'll pay. Eric, lead the way." With his claymore snug on his back and dirks sheathed at his wrists, he jogged through the darkened forest. His men followed, as silently as he through the dense brush.

The cold of night had fully descended and fog clung to the undergrowth. An hour in, he lifted a hand and called a soundless halt. Smoke. The scent pervaded the air.

"They're above on the rise, Captain." Eric gripped his knees, lugging in a breath from the fast pace they'd run.

"Aye, and MacLean wishes our arrival. He draws us to him with fire." He motioned to his men to huddle. Whispering, he warned, "Expect them to be prepared, very prepared. Fan out. We're close."

MacLean's guard would be out there. Although like phantoms in the night, his men slithered away, using the dark to their advantage. This was their land, and none knew it as they did.

He'd honor his word to Marie and protect her. Or die trying.

* * * *

Marie's heartbeat raced.

MacLean ordered the fire be lit then commanded a band of his men to head deeper into the forest, to circle around and take positions where they could to watch for Archie's warriors. Hands planted on his hips, MacLean smirked. "Are you content up there, lass?"

She would be if he hadn't tied her up the moment they'd arrived at camp. Bound and wedged within the high bow of a tree, she couldn't move for fear of toppling to the hard ground beneath. MacLean had smugly insisted he'd done this for her own good. It was safest for her if she remained out of harm's way. He'd even pocketed the dirk Archie had given her, and if she could spit out the foul-mouthed gag, she'd scream a warning. She'd never forgive herself if Archie got hurt. This was all her fault.

She glared at MacLean then the fire below. *Archie, don't you dare come. Don't you—*

A warrior burst into the clearing. "Chief, two bands of MacDonalds have arrived, one closely followed by the other." He gulped in air. "Our men have moved in behind the second band."

"How far away are they?"

"On the lower ridge."

So close. She was out of time. She shoved her roped hands

hard to the trunk and sawed while MacLean kicked dirt over the fire and doused it. A bare sliver of moonlight trickled through the thick canopy above.

MacLean withdrew his claymore and readied himself.

* * * *

On his belly, Archie slithered under a bush, taking the utmost care not to make a sound. Once through to the other side, he crouched. MacLean's men were everywhere. He'd maneuvered up the rise and deep into the midst of them without being spotted. He had to reach MacLean, or at least get as close as he could before he called his men to arms. That arrogant bastard would pay for taking Marie.

He held his position, scanned each direction. The moonlight filtered through, the acrid scent of smoke now gone. Slowly, carefully, he palmed his dirk, all his senses narrowed in on his left.

A shadow moved. One of MacLean's men. He caught the glint in his adversary's eye. Archie flung his weapon then sprang and caught the warrior as he fell to the ground, his dirk embedded deep between the man's eyes. An instant death. No noise. He dragged the fallen warrior to the closest scrub, pulled his dirk free then rolled the body underneath. MacLean wouldn't rule Islay, not on his watch, nor while he drew breath.

He slipped behind a thick trunk. Beyond, a clearing with a fire doused in the center, beckoned him.

The wait was over, and his blood roared for revenge.

* * * *

Marie stopped sawing as the forest went eerily quiet. It was as if even the creatures had taken refuge. A shadow passed at the base of a tree near the one she was wedged within. Archie. Every cell in her body was so attuned to him. He was here.

MacLean lifted his claymore high as he prepared to attack.

Her heartbeat hammered out of control.

"About time we meet again, MacLean." Archie's voice

rumbled low and deadly through the clearing, sending her pulse spiking even higher. One man would walk away from this battle alive, and it had to be Archie.

"I'm sorry, Katherine," she whispered into her gag. If MacLean died, then so did she and her sister. She should've tried harder to get Archie to listen to her.

"About time you got here, MacDonald. The Rhinns shall be mine afore this day is out. I've waited a long time for this moment."

"The Rhinns will never be yours." Archie edged around the clearing, keeping to the darkest corners. "And I shall prove it afore this day is out."

She remained perfectly still, not wanting to divert Archie's attention from the man who would take every advantage of it if she did.

"The Rhinns were lost by my father, but I shall see this land returned to me." Brow cocked, MacLean swung his sword as if readying himself. "How is my dear sister by the way?"

"Her wellbeing is of no concern of yours, nor has it been for over a decade. Cease the conversation, MacLean. 'Tis time to fight." Archie lifted his blade and let out a fierce battle cry. It rang in her ears then increased in crescendo as it boomed in every direction around her. His men were everywhere, but then so were MacLean's.

MacLean came at Archie. Their two great blades clashed dead center and sparked, and the brutal force of the strike sent Archie lurching back a step under the jarring impact. "There is naught I like more than an eager opponent," MacLean snarled.

"I'm the most eager adversary you'll find." Archie shoved against him. "Let's end this. Now." He struck MacLean, landing several hard blows. He fought to make ground.

"My men surround us, MacDonald." MacLean attacked aggressively to bring Archie into the play of moonlight, each of his hits stronger than the last. "Do you feel the itch in your back?

A dirk will soon be embedded deep within it."

"Watch for it yourself." Archie shot forward and landed a vicious blow on MacLean's left.

They fought, sweat pouring from their bodies. All around the sound of men grunting and fighting surged. She wanted to drown it all out as the cheers came from warriors who'd taken their opponent down. So many were dying. Clan MacLean or MacDonald?

And Archie fought for his life, the urge to kill MacLean clearly spurring him on. He would die before he ever gave up this land.

* * * *

The urge to kill throbbed through Archie as battle lust rode him hard. Each time one of his men felled a MacLean, their battle cheer rang loud and hastened his attack. "Your men fall, MacLean, and in far greater numbers than mine."

"You get ahead of yourself, MacDonald, as you did in leaving your faerie behind at the loch. A bad move." MacLean's gaze glinted with determination. "A curious wee lass she is to wish herself into the middle of this battle. She's so charming though, wouldnae you say?"

"I'll kill you if you've harmed her, and I'll make it as painful as possible."

"If she survives, I intend to keep her for myself. What say you, Marie?" MacLean searched the trees. "Is this battle all you'd hoped for? You can answer once I've killed your warrior if you prefer."

Damn the man. If Marie was up there, he wouldn't be able to aid her until he'd won this fight. He slammed his blade into MacLean's side.

Winded, MacLean grunted and fell back a step. "You'd attack a man as he looks upon the beauty of one of the fae? Shame on you, MacDonald."

"Then it'd pay for you to keep this fight between—"

A heavy thump sounded at the base of the tree. Marie was bound, gagged and fighting for a breath. In a flash, he slit her bindings and ripped the cloth free. "Breathe, my sweet."

She gulped in air, her gaze darting over his shoulder. "Behind—"

MacLean's sword blow knocked him onto his back and MacLean swung again. Archie grappled to meet the attack, their blades crashing inches from his nose. His arm shook as MacLean's blade drew closer toward his neck. One breath would see cold steel slicing into his throat.

"You appear to be in a predicament." MacLean sniggered and shoved down harder. "Does one's life flash afore their eyes as their death hovers?"

"You talk too much, MacLean." He kicked the man's shin then rolled as MacLean's blade nearly nicked his ear.

"Archie. I told you no scratches."

His woman was telling him off, now? For some reason, relief swept through him. Even a battle couldn't halt her fighting spirit.

"And I told you no entering the battle. We will have words, and very soon." He shot to his feet, barely ducking MacLean's next blow. "MacLean, only the lowest would use an innocent woman as you have."

"Had she remained where she was, she would still be safe. 'Tis now you who talks too much."

"Then our talking is over." Driven, Archie struck MacLean, landing one hard blow after another. With each strike, Marie cried out for him to cease, but he wouldn't give the man any quarter. Marie's demand for MacLean's capture was out. Death was his only option.

He slammed his blade home and MacLean stumbled to one knee. He slid his claymore tight against MacLean's throat. "Any last words, MacLean?"

"Even if I die, my men will continue to fight, and my son

will take my place."

"Then I'll see to his death as well." He pressed until blood oozed. "Although I believe we discussed this being painful."

"Archie." Marie rasped his name as she belly-crawled toward him. "I can't survive this if you kill him."

"Get back, Marie." Blood seeped from an open wound on her in the exact spot where he'd cut MacLean's neck.

"I'm not fae. I'm from the future. Kill him and you kill me. He's yet to father my paternal line."

"'Tis impossible."

"My sister deserves to live even if I don't. She had no part in this."

"I willnae concede defeat." He glared at MacLean and pressed deeper.

Marie screamed and blood streamed down and soaked her shirt.

He yanked his blade back. She couldn't be dying when only MacLean should, but damn it, she was. "Keep pressure on that cut."

"He has to live." She clasped her neck but blood still pulsed through.

MacLean made a grab for his dirk and Archie slammed him back to the ground. Marie moaned and bent over. Hell, he was still hurting her by beating MacLean.

He hauled the man by the scruff of his shirt toward the rope he'd bound Marie in then used it to bind him. Once divested of all his weapons, he raced back to Marie. "Hold still."

"I can't stop the bleeding." Her gaze flared with distress. "Please, you've got to help."

"I will. No one takes you from me." He ripped a strip from the hem of his shirt and tightened it around her neck.

"Take care of MacLean too. You might have to stop his bleeding as well. That could be it."

"You expect me to coddle my enemy?"

Gasping, she pointed to her wound. "Yes, and make it quick."

"Next you know, I'll be baking him an oatcake." He did the same for MacLean then returned to her.

"Well, there's no need to go that far." She chuckled, actually chuckled. His woman had no self-preservation.

He rechecked her injury, but the bleeding had slowed. "It looks better. How do you feel? Do you hurt anywhere else?"

"Everywhere." She dragged her shirt up and exposed a darkening bruise. "I never want to fall from a tree again. It really hurts."

Needing to hold her close, he cupped her face. "I never intended you any harm."

"I know, and this is my fault too." She kissed him, and he wanted to drown in her kiss, but the battle wasn't yet over.

"Why'd you go with MacLean?"

"I was out of choices. I'm sorry for disobeying your order."

"You'll never do so again. Can you move?" He scooped her up and set her on her feet, wanting only to smother her in his hold. "I dinnae care to leave you, but you must get back into that tree and out of harm's way."

"I'll go." She wobbled as she took a step. "I'm so sorry for what happened. I know this isn't the outcome you wanted, but"—her gaze softened as she looked at him—"thank you. I never had any doubt you'd come, even though I couldn't stand it. I'll make this all up to you somehow. I promise."

"Dinnae thank me yet. The battle isnae—"

"Archie." John burst through the trees and into the clearing, his gaze landing on MacLean then them. "We've subdued most of MacLean's men. A couple have turned tail. Eric is doing penance and chasing them." He strode forward and grasped his shoulder. "The battle is over."

"Over?" For years, he'd fought MacLean, and it would never be over until MacLean died in a battle on this very land before the turn of the century as Marie had stated.

His brother eyed MacLean. "Would you mind telling me why he still lives?"

"When I attempted to take his life, I almost took Marie's. He must live. The two are bound through her magic. Are you certain every MacLean has submitted?"

"It's over, brother. This day is ours. We've won this war."

Euphoria should be thrumming through him, but fear for Marie surged deep within. He'd almost caused her death because he'd never believed her. He'd never take such a risk again, never ignore any plea she made for him to listen. After dragging her against him, he held her in a viselike grip. "I cannae believe you're no' fae."

"I'm glad you finally believe me, just not how it came about," she mumbled into his shirtfront. "Does this mean I'm not in quite as much trouble as I could be?"

"Aye, I seek your forgiveness for almost taking your life."

"You're forgiven."

He tightened his hold on her then nodded at his brother. "She's no' from this time, and in the future MacLean breeds her paternal line."

"That's going to make things difficult."

"More than difficult." He released Marie then stormed across to MacLean. "You'll be taken back to Dunyvaig. You owe your life to your progeny, for if I had my way, your blood would be soaking into this ground."

He'd finally come face to face with his enemy, but instead of seeing to his mission, he was taking him captive. Winning this war had now taken a turn and his next decision would have to be made with great care.

"It'll be okay." Marie caught his hand and slid her fingers into his. "We have the fae on our side, the most mischievous imps around. I can handle a Highland warrior, no matter how stubborn you are."

He wished to be one with his faerie, to hold her for all time. Wishes. They were so damn frustrating.

Chapter 10

Marie tramped across the sandy beach toward the moored birlinns. Golden grains sparkled under the rising sun. It would be a stunner of a day. If only every inch of her didn't ache. She desperately needed to rest.

At least they'd won. Well, she'd won.

Archie stomped ahead of her, prodding MacLean to walk faster. His relief had soon turned to frustration.

"This will all turn out okay, Archie." How many times had she said that these past few hours?

"His life is damn well tied to yours." He snorted. "That's no' what I call working it out."

"Dinnae mind him. He needs some time to calm. No' much farther." John wrapped an arm around her shoulders, and she leaned into him, grateful for his support. "'Tis been my brother's lifelong wish to see to MacLean's death, although it is what it is, and we must accept the outcome."

"John, take your hands off my woman." Archie glared at him.

"She needs aid and rest, and I dinnae see you offering any. Quit the black mood." John bent to her ear. "He's impossible sometimes."

"So I've learnt." She winked at John, glad for his camaraderie. "And obstinate, which is something I really need to work on weaning out of him. Do you think it's achievable?"

"Nay, I've been trying to drive his stubbornness from him for years." He grinned. "Why dinnae you tell me of the future, of this place you're from? I'm already rather taken with how strong the women are. Your fighting spirit is commendable."

"Where I come from, women know how to stand up for themselves, and your fighting spirit is rather commendable too."

"Thank you, lass. 'Tis an interesting concept of a woman standing up for herself. Does a man no' have to prove what he can offer? I have lands on Argyll, a small parcel, but 'tis all mine if you wish to consider me over my impossible brother."

"Oooh, you have your own lands? Keep talking. I like the idea of a man with—"

"Enough." Archie stopped.

"But he has land," she continued to tease.

"I have more." To John, he snapped, "Go find your own woman. This one is mine." He grabbed her, tossed her over his shoulder then stormed along the beach past the moored birlinns. She giggled, enjoying his strong-arm attention even though she shouldn't have goaded him to it.

"Hey, where are we going, Mr. Highlander?"

"John can see to our captive."

"That doesn't tell me where we're going. Put me down. I promise I'll stop teasing you."

"You're coming with me. Somewhere private where I can show you exactly how you're mine."

"Well, now that sounds even more promising than the lands."

She bumped along over his shoulder until he reached the seaward entrance of the loch. Carefully, he set her on her feet then hand in hand, they tramped a half mile across the beach to the north. Along the way, Archie collected twigs and driftwood, and after finding a nice sheltered hollow in the dunes, he laid his armful down. With enough wood for a fire, he dug a hole, pulled off the stringy dried bark and over it, struck a small piece of flint with his dirk. Breathing on the sparks, he coaxed them to life. He added wood and brought the fire to a crackling blaze.

"I'm going to catch us something to eat." He tipped up her chin, planted a hard kiss on her lips. "No' only do I have land, but I can provide all you'll ever need."

"You don't have to prove yourself to me." No, but she didn't mind if he wished to try. She liked seeing him like this, deep in his element. "Is there anything I can do to help?"

"There's a brook. Wash up then rest." He unpinned his plaid over his shirt and trews and spread it before the fire. "I willnae be long."

The stream gurgled into the sea. Washing up sounded wonderful. She ambled along the shore. On her knees, she splashed her face and hands, removing the blood and grime from her skin. MacLean had bleed as she had, their lives tied together. Archie had said they were going to take the man back to Dunyvaig, but more than that, she needed to ensure he handed MacLean over to the king. It was the only way to make sure history remained on course. He had to agree. He'd come so far.

And so had they, together.

From the moment he'd dragged her from the faerie circle, their bond had deepened. Once he'd touched her, kissed her, sent her soaring far beyond her body, she'd longed for him in a way she'd never expected. Their lives were entwined, and with far more than just his wish. He believed her, and she didn't want to waste a moment of whatever precious time they had left.

A cackle of noise sounded from farther downstream. Archie rounded the corner, splashing through the shallows and swinging a goose by its hind legs. In the depths of the wild, he was in his element. She loved being this close to him, seeing him like this.

"Nice catch." She patted the spot beside her.

"How are you feeling? Still sore?" He sat, plunged his feet into the water and cleaned the goose.

"I'll heal." She kicked off her boots, dipped her feet next to his then leaned her head against his shoulder. "I could sleep for a week after today though."

"You can if you wish, although in my bed." His voice was husky and low. "I now have an even greater fear of leaving you behind." He washed his hands and face as she had done then tugged her to her feet. "Let's go warm up afore the fire and cook this goose."

Back at their cozy camp, she tucked herself close to the fire. The sun blazed high, but the wind chilled her. Archie busied himself fashioning a spit. Before long, the meat roasted over the brilliant orange and red flames.

She shouldn't be enjoying herself this much, not considering how many had lost their lives, and only a few miles away, but they had survived. Islay was safe from MacLean. The villagers would no longer live in fear, and neither would Mary or James.

"You appear deep in thought." On the tartan, Archie relaxed on his side.

"I was just thanking my lucky stars."

"There is no luck in the stars, only in the fae." He slid her hair over her shoulder. "Even though I know you're no longer one of the little folk, they still sent you to me."

She looked deep into his eyes, his belief lightening her heart. "I've longed for this conversation. Everything I've ever told you has been the truth."

"I'll never fail to believe your word again." He leaned in and nuzzled her neck, right above the binding over her wound.

"I'm glad my sister made her wish. I've never had so much adventure, and I wouldn't have missed this for the world, all the tension and trouble included."

"Aye, but I may prefer a less spirited woman." He took her

mouth in a soft kiss, one so tender she melted against him. "Or more biddable."

"Liar." She pushed him onto his back, slung her leg over his groin and straddled him. Oh, he was hard, very hard, and they were separated by no more than their clothes. "Now you believe me, do you also believe I told you the truth about being protected?"

"From getting with child?" He cupped her face and drew her mouth back to his. He kissed her again, long and slowly. "Aye, 'tis all I can think about."

"Me too." She wound her fingers into his dark shoulder-length locks touched with gold. Sinking into him, she wanted more. "I'm hungry, Archie. Show me what it's like to join as one."

* * * *

Archie wanted Marie with a thirst he'd never known. He'd longed for her every moment of their separation.

Still, he should slow things down, and he would if Marie's soft little moans weren't driving every thought from his head. Kissing her, tasting the warm honey of her mouth had his cock trying to spear through his trews. He gripped her arms and enforced a little distance. "Hold."

"I can't." She rocked against him, stirring him further. 'Twas too much. He rolled her onto her back and rose over top of her. "Touch me, anywhere, somewhere. Please, Archie. I don't want to go slow."

Heaven help him, he didn't either. He palmed her breast through the soft linen of her shirt until she arched fully into him.

"That feels so good." Her eyes begged him for more. "Kiss me."

He swept his tongue inside her mouth, the need to touch all of her riding him hard. He wanted to trace every inch of her smooth skin with his hands and tongue. He fumbled with the hem of her shirt then dragged it over her head and freed her perfect breasts. Cupping their fullness, he gorged himself on the sight. "I want to eat you."

"Yes, please."

He thumbed her peaking nipples then slid his tongue over the first one. Divine, and naught could stop him from pulling her fully into his mouth.

He feasted on her before moving onto her other breast and laving it with equal attention.

"That feels amazing." She panted as she clung to him.

"Aye, my faerie has boundless magic and has ensnared me beyond distraction." He gripped her trews and tugged them down until she lay bared to his gaze. Her creamy skin flushed with a healthy glow, and the place between her thighs glistened. She was already wet, and his tongue tingled for a taste. "You're so beautiful, Marie. I want to make you come, over and over."

"I want that too, but together."

Blood pounding, he lowered his head and covered her mouth with his. He kissed her, allowing his passion its full release. He would make sure she experienced naught but sheer pleasure as he claimed her. No more would she hurt.

* * * *

Completely consumed by Archie, Marie couldn't keep her hips from pushing against his. He'd awakened her body and stamped his possession into her bones. She was his. She grasped his broad shoulders, skimmed down his arms and over his thick forearms. So big and strong, he moved from her mouth to her neck. He dropped a soft kiss over her wound then trailed down the valley of her breasts.

Hot and hard, he surrounded her, building her passion to a pinnacle with one long stroke of his tongue after another. "I want to touch you too."

"Later." He caressed the inside of her thigh then nudged his knee between hers. All her nerves teetered on the edge as he swept his hand over the part of her craving him and his hard cock.

He pushed his finger deep inside. Exquisite pleasure radiated out and she couldn't hold back her moan.

"Marie, I need to prepare you first."

"You've been doing that for days. I'm fully prepared, so don't hold back." She stared into the glorious depths of his passion-flared gaze. He stroked her, hard and fast, until a powerful whirlpool of need flared within her.

"Let go," he whispered.

"No, I want to do this together. It's time. Make me yours in every way."

* * * *

"Aye, in every way." Archie's mind went dark with lust. "Together."

She glided her hands down his sides and brushed over his erection. With the softest caress, she explored his length over the leather covering him. Such friction. She would send him over the edge before he was ready. "I want you, inside of me, right where you belong."

His heartbeat hammered out of control.

"Now." She slid his belt free, dragged open his trews and encircled him. He fought his need to move, to explode in her hand as she stroked his shaft, her thumb swiping seductively over the head. "I want you to be the man who takes me first. No other but you."

Hell, he wanted it too. He shucked off his clothes. No more could he delay, and with his hands on her hips, he lifted her to him and moved between her legs. He teased his cock along her slick folds. "Open wider for me."

She spread her legs farther. "I know they'll be a little pain. I can handle it, but don't stop."

Covering her mouth with his, he demanded a response that would distract her mind. Then he pushed against her thin barrier. This was the moment he'd never thought he'd have with her, and now he couldn't hold back. He tore through her innocence and plunged deep inside her hot channel.

She smiled against his lips, clutched his butt and urged him to go faster. "Make me yours."

He kissed her, pounding harder, deeper, until she consumed him. Her soft moans encouraged him, and he took her frantically, unable to hold back.

"So good." She raked his back then screamed his name.

He was lost as her inner muscles tightened and dragged him in. His thoughts flew and his release exploded violently along with hers. Deep within, he spilled his seed.

A perfect surrender, a moment like no other.

"My woman," he whispered as he slumped on top of her, completely spent. "For as long as I can keep you. I wish for no other."

* * * *

Archie slowly lifted himself from her and cool air swept Marie's damp skin. Her limbs had gone to mush, but she pushed open her eyes and grinned at his satisfied smile. "We need to do that again, my Highlander."

Powerful magic passed between them as he'd come inside her. She was his first, as he was hers, but she wanted more.

"Are you all right? I didnae hurt you too greatly?"

"No, and that was incredible. I had no idea it would be quite like that." She stroked his back, running her fingers over his corded muscles.

"If I'm too heavy, tell me." His breath tickled her ear.

"It would hurt more if you weren't where you are."

He rocked his hips and his shaft stirred and lengthened again inside her. "I never want to leave your body."

"Then don't." She sighed as he continued to rise and fill her. "This feels so good, so right."

"I would like to love you, all day and all night." His sensual words sent a thrill through her. He kissed her, taking her places she more than desired. He stroked deep inside, as if touching the very heart of her. "I want whatever time we have together to never end."

"As do I, Archie."

He increased his rhythm, slid his hand between her folds and rubbed her clit.

She moaned as she arched against him, moving with him as another orgasm built.

"I need to hear you scream my name." He drew his long length in and out, his kisses matching the ebb and flow of below. Then with one decisive flick of his finger over her nub, he made her come, so staggeringly fast.

She convulsed around him, crying out his name as he'd wished. She rode the waves, crashing hard as he roared and sank balls-deep inside her. His seed shot to her womb, and joined as one, a more perfect moment she'd never known.

"You distract me beyond my endurance, lass." He kissed her, stroking her sides as he rocked gently inside her. With a tender touch, he slowly brought them both back down.

She caught his face, looked deep into his eyes. "And I'll never let you forget it. Love me, Archie. I want more."

Chapter 11

Archie dragged himself away from Marie's warmth under the plaid he'd wrapped around them. So many hours he'd spent loving her.

"Where are you going?" Her seductive tone was achingly sweet, causing his cock to twitch with life.

"The goose is well and truly cooked." He nabbed it and returned to her side. "Are you hungry?"

"Exceedingly." She winked. "I told you that before."

"Imp. What will I do with you?" He tore off a chunk of meat, slipped the morsel between her lips then took a bite for himself. She looked so beautiful, the sun's late afternoon rays catching the golden strands in her hair and lighting them to brilliance. Her cheeks were flushed, her blue eyes twinkling with mischief. "What are you thinking?"

"Of nothing but you."

"You too consume my thoughts." He kissed the corner of her mouth then licked along her lower lip. "I never want that to change."

"You have such a way with words. Stubborn yet sweet." She glanced at the horizon. "When do we have to go back?"

"Afore one of my men come searching for us."

"And when will that be?"

"The tide will soon be high, and they'll wish to sail for Dunyvaig." He continued to feed her, ensuring she'd eaten her fill before polishing off the remainder of their meal.

"We need to talk about MacLean then." She tugged her shirt on, shimmied into her breeches and covered every delectable inch. "Even though I'm not fae, I've always believed I needed to fulfill your wish before I can return home to Katherine. To win this war, you need to hand MacLean over to the king."

He dragged on his clothes, his gut clenching at her request. Worse, though, she'd yet to steer him wrong, which meant he was doomed to go along with her plan.

"Archie, MacLean is an integral part of all this. You know as well as I do the king wants the three chiefs involved in this feud to atone for their behavior. He already has two of them, and I believe once he has MacLean, he'll be able to fully address his concerns with them." She laid a hand on his arm, her soothing touch easing some of his frustration. "This dispute has raged for years, and only one man can now bring about a difference. Let the king do what he's supposed to do. Rule."

"'Tis no' the—"

'I know. I know. 'Tis no' the Highlander way," she said. "But please, at least consider what I'm asking. Angus MacDonald, Donald MacDonald and Lachlan MacLean are all at fault here. They've caused such havoc." She scooted onto his lap, wrapped her arms around his neck. "I'm counting on you to keep a level head and agree. You've had your vengeance for MacLean's attack on the village and he's lost a large number of men. The battle between the clans has to stop."

Damn it. He understood her reasoning. He just didn't care for it.

"Please, say you agree."

"'Tis only a matter of time afore MacLean's men regroup

and attempt another assault. He will have a second who'll come for him, and if MacLean remains in my dungeons, I'll have a bargaining chip."

"Bargaining chip aside, this is about keeping history on course. You have to follow through with my plan. I've learnt so much at Mary's hand, and once added to what I already knew, I haven't a doubt this is the right move." She brushed her nose against his. "What else do I need to say to convince you?"

"I've learnt fae or no', your magic is strong. I will consider what you ask, but only consider."

"Thank you. It's a start. I can see it's going to take me some time to work out all your bad kinks. I'll get there though. Just watch me." She kissed him, one hot kiss he wished could go on all day, except she pulled back and smiled. "Now take me home. I want to bounce around on a soft mattress and experience every pleasure you have to offer."

"I wish to explore, to leave no part of you untouched." He launched to his feet, taking her with him. Aye, he would seek every treasure her body held and uncover it.

* * * *

Marie raced up the sand dunes and stopped at the top. The tide was high, the anchored birlinns bobbing off shore. What a beautiful sight. Soon they'd be home. Hmm, when had Dunyvaig become home to her? She certainly missed Mary and James. Having kin close mattered.

Archie stepped in behind her, one arm sliding around her waist as he pulled her back to his chest. She wriggled her bottom against his groin and he groaned. "Take care, lass. I need to be able to walk from here to the galley."

She grinned. "Well, if you need aid, you know who to ask."

"Behave." He nipped her ear with his teeth.

"You need to take your own advice."

He grinned and waved to his brother as John strode toward them. "Archie, you're looking hearty and hale. I see your black mood has lifted."

"Aye, a little rest goes a long way. What of our men and MacLean's?"

"The dead have been buried and the injured tended to. Their loss has been significant, and of course our men wish to return, to celebrate our victory with our clan."

"We'll set sail. There's no need to delay."

"Good." John slapped his back. "Let's be away."

Archie lifted her into his arms, waded through the shallows and swung her into his boat as John boarded the other birlinn.

She raced to the stern, planted her hands on her hips and bellowed, "We sail for Dunyvaig. Hurry up and get this ship moving. That's an order, men."

Archie chuckled as he joined her. "You wish to captain my vessel?"

"I wish to get home and offer my endless aid as I've promised I would."

"Aye, and I willnae stop you." He kissed her then turned to his men. "Islay is ours, and no MacLean will ever defeat us. Hoist the sail and do as my lady bids."

Cheers abounded, and at the front of the birlinn, bound and gagged, MacLean grumbled.

Oh yes, there was nothing better than sailing the seas. They cruised out of Loch Gruinart, freedom now theirs.

As they journeyed around the coast, the sun dipped along the horizon and sent a final flare of red across the sky. Night fell. So beautiful. Even the moon, a bright ball of glorious orange, hung low, guiding their way home.

She nestled against Archie as a round of hearty songs rang out from his men. This was as it should be, and she was one step closer to getting back to her sister. The thought brought a moment of joy, until her heart heaved at the thought of leaving Archie. This was their time, but it wouldn't be for long. Still, she'd make every moment left to them count.

"We're almost home." Archie wrapped an arm around her shoulders, warding off the evening chill.

"Yes, home."

They rounded the tip of The Oa, the wind so favorable they shot across the water toward Lagavulin Bay with speed.

Before long, the massive stone walls of Dunyvaig beckoned with its strength. From the narrow tower windows, light glowed in welcome. Their clan awaited their return.

"Hell." Archie heaved to his feet.

A war galley approached fast from the north. Such a powerful ship with two masts, one in the center and one at the stern flying the King of Scotland's flag. Hell was right. She jumped up. "They must be searching for MacLean. What are you going to do?"

"I shouldnae be surprised they've come this far south." He grasped her hand and pressed it against his chest. "I dinnae care to hand him over."

"You have to. Please, it's the right thing to do. The king has a far greater force, an entire army at his disposal. You'll never win a fight against him." And surely, he couldn't think to take on the king's men at sea.

"Highlanders fight for what is theirs." He looked deep into her eyes then groaned. "Damn it. I cannae risk your life again, no' while you're on board. I've no choice."

"No, you're doing what's best for your clan, Once MacLean is in the king's hands, negotiations will get underway and a resolution found. You must see that."

He kissed her, so tenderly. "I dinnae wish to lose you."

"You never will." She touched her chest. "I'll always hold you close."

"Captain," Eric shouted. "What's your order?"

"Make berth. 'Tis time for MacLean to atone for his warring. The king shall have his way."

They crested the white-capped waves and skimmed the

waters into the bay. From atop the battlements, a shout was hailed from one guardsman to another.

Archie steered her to the bow then handed her over to one of his warriors. "Escort her inside. Immediately."

Archie's guardsman led Marie into the keep.

* * * *

When Archie had made his wish, his mind had been set on winning the war against MacLean. His wish shouldn't have brought him and Marie so close. Her very essence had become branded into his soul. By her deeds and desires, she'd woven her own spell around his heart, and he wasn't sure he'd be able to let her go when the time came.

He found his chamber window. There, darkened and cold. He thumped one foot as he waited then released a long breath as a light from within flickered to life. She was safe, and waiting for him.

"Archie." John bounded from his moored vessel onto the stone steps beside him. "What's your decision?"

"'Tis time to hand our captive over." In the birlinn, MacLean straightened from his sagged position at the bow then narrowed his gaze on the war galley sailing into the bay. The fearsome chief was helpless to change the course of the unfolding events, as was he.

"Are you certain? What of Angus?"

"This is a day of victory, and he will hear of it. That willnae be forgotten." He faced Eric. "Unbind MacLean's feet and bring him. He must walk toward his destiny."

"Aye, Captain." Eric unknotted MacLean's roped ankles, heaved him up then handed him across.

Archie seized MacLean's arm and marched him to the end of the sea-gate.

The war galley came into moor, and the ship's captain leapt onto the landing in his finely cut uniform. He tugged the dark cuffs of his coat as he passed his narrowed gaze over MacLean.

"You are the very man we've been searching for." He eyed Archie. "The king requests the Chief of MacLean's presence in Edinburgh, in whatever state we must bring him in. Although, I'm surprised to see he still stands alive in your hands, after what the villagers north of here have told me."

"We're no' barbarians. Take him, but if he ever steps foot on Islay again, his death will be assured."

The king's man motioned his second to come forward. "Take Lachlan MacLean and bind him to the center mast. Keep a guard on him at all times." He turned back to Archie. "I'm Captain Hugh Lindsay."

"Archie MacDonald." He crossed his arms. "MacLean attempted to take the Rhinns on our western coastline. He was unsuccessful."

"Another attack. I'm no' surprised. The king will be pleased though to hear of your willingness in handing MacLean over. I understand your predicament."

Willingness? Nay. 'Twas all Marie's doing. She alone had achieved such an outcome. He nodded at Captain Lindsay, eager to see him gone and off MacDonald land. "If there is naught more you need…"

"Nay, we must be away. Thank ye." The captain dipped his head and rejoined his men.

John grasped his shoulder. "'Tis the right thing to do, and none will gainsay your decision. This is certainly a day which will go down in history."

"Aye, even though I wish it differently." The king's men pushed away from their mooring and hoisted their sails.

"Speaking of wishes." John stroked his jaw. "It seems a woman from the future has cast a very decided spell over you. You've changed your mind then? The man who said he'd never take a woman as his."

"She's mine, but her future is elsewhere." He strode along the steps and up the trail.

John fell into step beside him. "Archie, Mother never had a midwife to tend her during her labor. Eventually you must set your worries aside. Life cannae be lived so."

"Dinnae tell me how to live my life."

"All women wish for bairns."

"I know, but 'tis a moot point since my woman willnae be here to bear them." He marched through the entrance. "She'll soon return to where she came from. I wish only for her to remain safe in her own time."

"That is no' what you wish for, and I willnae believe otherwise."

"I wish for her to live, to have a long life."

"Aye, but what of you? You want her. 'Tis clear to see."

"My heart bleeds for more, but this is one fight I will never win."

* * * *

What a bittersweet moment. Marie stood at the narrow window while below, Archie and John strode in. The king's war galley sailed into the dark with Lachlan MacLean aboard. She'd done it. Fulfilled Archie's wish, or at least as far as she could manage. Angus's release was now in his own hands. And that was how it should be, what history had foretold.

Surely soon, she'd now return home.

Tears misted her gaze as she searched the faerie circle. On the center stone a glimmer of moonlight sparkled off Mary's amulet. The sacred circle remained untouched. Even the grass was still, though it rippled in the breeze beyond. Such a place of magic, where the fae played, and where she would await the return of the veil.

"Marie." Mary pushed the door open, clutched her emerald skirts and raced toward her. "I heard. Lachlan lives and we won the battle."

"Yes, all is well." She hugged Mary, and her tears fell.

"'Twill be all right." Mary cupped her cheeks. "The men

said you were in the heart of it all."

"It couldn't be helped. Your brother was rather insistent I join him, not that I would've wanted it any other way. I live now because I was there."

"You've seen to Archie's wish then." Tears gathered in Mary's eyes too. "I'm going to miss you."

"I'll miss you too." She tugged Mary to the window. "Your amulet lies on the stone, but promise me—"

"Aye, you've already asked, and it shall be done. When you sailed for Loch Gruinart, I searched my trunk. I found my amulet, yet somehow there are two. I have a feeling you first told me the truth, that you're from the future, and you're my direct kin." Mary kissed her cheek. "Is it true?"

"Yes. Thank you for believing me." She squeezed Mary hard, not wanting to let go. "I'm so grateful the fae brought me here, that I met you, and came to know Archie."

"You'll miss him?"

"With my heart and soul." The circle beckoned though. Katherine had to be close. "My sister is all I have left. She would never give up waiting for me, as I'll never give up trying to return to her. She's my twin. We came into this world together, and will always remain so. I love her."

"Excuse me, my ladies." A maid knocked on the opened door, dipped her head toward Mary. "The tub ye ordered is ready. The lads would like to bring it in."

"Good. Come in, boys." Mary motioned them forward and they lugged the tub in. Eyeing her, she added, "I thought you'd like to refresh yourself."

"I'd love it." Mary was so thoughtful.

The lads filled the bath with pails of steaming water. Mary took a bottle of scented oil from one of the maids and added a few drops to the bathwater. The air swirled with the delicate scent of white roses. What a treat.

Another servant arrived with a trencher and placed it on

Archie's side table. After pulling up a chair, Marie cut a wedge from one of the prime cuts of beef and popped it into her mouth. It was seasoned just right, as were the roasted vegetables. Delicious. "I feel totally spoilt."

"Here's some wine." Mary passed her a goblet. "Would you like help readying yourself for your bath?"

Below-stairs the raucous sound of the clan in full cheer traveled to her. "No, you go and enjoy the festivities. This is a night for celebration."

"Relax and rest then." She backed out of the room and closed the door behind her.

She wanted nothing more, and after taking a few sips of wine, she shucked her clothes. Breathing a long sigh, she slid into the water. Heav-en-ly.

After dunking her head, she came up and found Archie standing inside the room, his eyes a blaze of molten gold. "I believe this is the first time you've actually obeyed my orders and I've found you where you're supposed to be."

"Yes, but I can't guarantee a second time. Enjoy the moment while it lasts. Are you joining me?"

"Nay, my bed awaits." Grinning, he tossed his shirt aside. His rippling abs and tanned pecs gleamed under the dancing firelight. Then her warrior slid his pants down his thighs and off. "I want your heart racing against mine. I ache for it."

"You wish for me to ease your pain?" She rose from the tub, grabbed the drying cloth and wrapped it around her. She couldn't get to him fast enough.

"Aye, but with every inch of your beautiful body within my sight." He flicked off the cloth, scooped her up and lowered her onto his mattress. "I want to love you, right through the night."

"Yes, please." She stroked the soft brown and blue patchwork blanket. "Fast. Slow. However you like."

"I want it all." Lust filled his gaze as he slid his knees between her thighs and widened her legs. "But only within you, where I belong."

"Ahh, finally we're speaking the same language. It took a while." She pushed her fingers deep into his hair and held onto him. "I love that you know where you belong."

"You were mine from the first moment I laid eyes on you." He rubbed his hard cock over her folds, teasing her clit. "I would wish for you again and again if I could."

"As would"—she gasped as he plunged into her—"I."

Pleasure overflowed her body as tingles raced across her skin, leaving no part of her untouched. Buried deep inside her, their connection moved beyond all time. "I never want to be parted from you again."

"Aye, and I wish I could have a thousand more wishes." He rode her hard, and then kissed her until her orgasm built and she reached that divine pinnacle she loved. "Each wish would be to make you come, to have you calling my name as I took you."

"Archie." She screamed his name as she clasped his butt and pushed her hips toward him. She flew, her inner muscles gripping and dragging him home.

"My faerie." He looked deep into her eyes then roared as came right along with her, his seed shooting straight to her core.

They were joined, in the most elemental way, she and her Highlander from another time. "Yes, your faerie. Always yours," she whispered as he collapsed on top of her.

* * * *

Marie cupped Archie's face then stirred him awake with a gentle kiss. "You're heavy."

"Sorry, love. You make me lose my mind." He eased up a touch then rocked gently inside her. "A very contented mind."

She stretched and smiled. "I think it's my turn on top."

He reveled in where their bodies met, and his cock twitched and lengthened again, always hungry for more. He nuzzled between her beautiful breasts. "I shouldnae have neglected these sweet morsels. Your turn on top will have to wait."

"Neglecting is—" She moaned as he drew her nipple deep into his mouth and sucked. "Oh, bad. Very bad."

Throughout the night, he didn't make that mistake again. He savored every single inch of her, and she returned the favor, loving him as he loved her. They were the most magical hours, and he fell asleep as the first rays of dawn stole across the sky, his woman cocooned safely within his arms.

Such peace invaded his soul.

* * * *

Marie dragged herself from the bed as Archie's breathing evened out. She would never leave the temptation of his body if she didn't attempt it now.

She searched his trunk and discovered her clothing laundered and folded neatly within. After dressing in her white linen pants, camisole and silk shirt, she nabbed her fine woolen coat and slunk out of his chamber.

Even as her heart heaved, she crept down the winding stairs and around the edge of the great hall, taking care not to awaken the men sprawled across pallets before the hearth. Katherine needed her, would be waiting for her. It was all that kept her moving.

Outside, she snuck across the stony courtyard and passed under the arched entrance.

The faerie circle remained quiet, bare of any breeze, and the amulet upon the center stone beckoned her to come.

She slipped between the two perimeter stones and knelt before Mary's talisman. "I'm here, Katherine. Where are you?"

A breeze made her hair tickle her face. She closed her eyes, hoping the faeries were at play. "Please, let Katherine come," she cried to them.

Her sister was close. Every cell in her body sensed it. She should take the amulet and make a—

"I'm here." Katherine's voice whispered all around her.

She sagged onto the stone. "I saw to Archie's wish."

"I knew you would." Another wisp of air brushed her cheek. "Come home to me."

"Marie!" Archie shouted her name as he raced down the trail, his white shirttails flying free behind him.

"Ahh, your Highland warrior comes." Katherine's voice curled with mischief.

"Marie!" He hit the edge of the circle, bounced off and slammed onto the ground. Stunned, he shook his head then staggered to his feet. "Hell, the veil's up."

"Marie, take the amulet," her sister crooned.

She patted her hands through the air, searching for her.

"Is she in there with you?" Archie shoved against the veil. "Dinnae go to her, no' yet. I need to hold you, one last time."

"Sis, every day since you disappeared into the past, I've returned and waited for you," Katherine revealed. "I'm right here, and I've watched those ruins and wished for the castle to reappear. Pick up the amulet. It must be the only way you can get back to me."

Yes, she had to get back to Katherine. "I don't want to leave him, but I'll never leave you." Archie's eyes had darkened, losing all light. "I have to go," she pleaded to him.

He thumped his chest. "I love you."

"I can't live without my sister."

"I would never ask you to. Pick up the talisman." His voice broke. "Go to her."

Hands shaking, she slowly reached for it. She could do this. She had to. She wrapped her fingers around it and slipped it over her head. "I love you too, Archie."

A rumble of thunder boomed and her Highlander slithered to his knees. "Guardians of Dunyvaig," he rasped. "Keep my loved one safe."

"Marie." Katherine shimmered into view and grabbed her. "Oh my goodness, you're back."

Hot tears scorched her cheeks as she clung to Katherine.

"We're together again."

"You truly love him?" Katherine searched her gaze.

"Yes. Knowing him has been a moment of magic, an adventure unlike any I've ever known." Keeping hold of Katherine, she staggered to the edge of the circle. They were still between times, and Archie was beyond her reach, but there. She slumped to her knees, not losing her grip on her sister who dropped down beside her. "He stole my heart with one simple wish."

"He said he loves you, Marie. How can you leave him?" Anguish crossed her sister's face.

"Archie!" John raced down the trail. "What's happened?"

"She's gone." Archie clutched the grass then ripped handfuls free. "She's gone."

John lowered to his knees. "Then wish for her back, as you wished for her in the very beginning."

"This is what she wanted, and I willnae make her choose between her sister and me." He seized his brother's arm. "I must give her up."

Katherine squeaked. "Oh my goodness. He really does love you."

Yes, but her Highlander was lost to her for all time.

"We have to find a way to get to him." Katherine tugged on her hand.

"It's impossible."

"Nothing is ever impossible. C'mon, Marie, neither of us have anything tying us to the future except each other. If you've traveled to the past using the amulet, then why can't it happen again? Don't you remember my wish? It was for both of us to find a moment of magic, to live and to have a ton of adventure along the way." She swiped the talisman from around Marie's neck, joined their hands together and wound it around both their wrists. "Let's do this, sis, but this time, together. You're not leaving me again."

"The clans will always be at war."

"Yes, but they're our clans, and you know as well as I do how hard it's been without Mum. Do you want to lose another person you love too?"

"No, I want him." Everything within her cried out to return to him. "Are you sure?"

"Yes. When one finds love, one should never let it go. I want to do this."

"But how?" Before her, Archie pressed his hand against the barrier and she settled her hand over his. He was so close, yet so far away. "He's still beyond my reach."

"Do you hear that, John? Whispers from within." Archie looked straight at her, and her heart near flew right out of her chest.

"He can hear me. Archie," she cried.

"I heard." John gaped. "Marie calls for you."

"John." Katherine thumped the veil. "It's Katherine, Marie's sister. Tell Archie to make a wish, for both my sister and me."

John pressed his hand over Katherine's as if he knew exactly where she was. "Make a wish, brother, for both of them. Katherine asked it."

Archie blew out a breath. "Are you sure, Marie? What if this doesnae work?"

"We have to try. Please, make the wish."

He squeezed his eyes shut. "Aye, I shall try. Guardians of Dunyvaig, I ask for a wish, for you to send me the woman who has stolen my heart and the one she holds closest to her. Bring them here, so we need never live apart again." He swept his hand through the air and her amulet rose, breached the barrier and spun into his palm. He snapped his eyes open, locked his gaze on her amulet.

A wind rose and tunneled around, whipping her hair across her face. She grasped hold of Katherine, ensuring the amulet was bound tight around them both. "Don't let go of me, sis. If you do, you'll be in more trouble than it's worth."

"I'm holding on. Sisters, forever."

"Come to me, my love." Archie jerked on her amulet.

She fell through the barrier and against the very warrior who awaited her.

Katherine was plastered against John. They'd done it. They were here.

She unraveled the talisman and threw her arms around Archie's neck. "I missed you."

"Unbelievable." He grinned. "My faerie returns."

Katherine stared at John then brushed the sides of her red and blue woolen coat. "I'm Katherine. Nice to meet you."

"John, and 'tis a pleasure to meet you." He kissed her hand.

Archie lifted Marie to her feet and swung her into his arms. "You're home."

"I'm home." She laughed as he spun her about. "Goodness, I loved your wish."

"I intend to make many more." He set her on her feet then lowered to one knee. "And I'll begin with the greatest wish I have. Marie MacLean, I cannae live without you. You hold my heart and soul in your hands." He brought her hands to his lips and kissed her fingers. "I wish to take you as my wife, to love you as a man should love his woman. Will you do me the great honor of marrying me?"

"What about bairns?" She dropped to her knees. "I want them, and for you to give them to me."

"Then 'twill be done. I'd rather have love than never have it at all." He kissed her, just as she'd longed for.

She was here and never leaving him.

"Yes, then I wish for a lifetime with you."

Wishes. They were what one made of them, and now she was back in his arms, all her wishes come true.

Chapter 12

On the upper dunes north of Loch Gruinart, Marie knelt behind Archie, massaging his shoulders. This was their place, where they'd first joined fully after the battle. The cloudless sky blazed brilliant blue, and inside, her heart overflowed with so much love.

"I can't believe we're here." She slid her hands around his neck and leaned against the heat of his bare back. "I thought your clansmen would never let us leave Dunyvaig for our honeymoon."

A week past, he'd made her his wife beside the faerie circle which had brought them together, Katherine by her side, and John by his.

"They've seen how I lose track of time when I'm alone with you. I cannae blame them." He half-turned, slid an arm around her waist and swept her onto his lap. "And I shall lose even more time now since you wear naught but my shirt."

"I like wearing your shirts. You may loan them to me whenever you wish."

His golden eyes heated to a smoldering hue. "I wish to love you."

"And I wish for a Highland warrior who knows exactly

where to sheath his blade."

Grinning, he slipped his hands under her shirttails and caressed her bare bottom.

Intense emotions swamped her. "Don't ever let me go."

"Never." He kissed her, long and deeply, with breathless seduction.

Every inch of her throbbed.

"Make all my wishes come true, Archie."

"I vow to make it my lifelong mission."

Oh, yes. Missions. They were what she now thrived on, and together they were about to undertake the most important one of their lives.

Their quest?

To be bound to one another for all time.

Author's Note

The ruins of Dunyvaig Castle holds such history within its crumbled stone walls, a past I find completely fascinating. I thoroughly enjoyed reading the accounts told of the Highlander clans who lived on the Isle of Islay and neighboring Jura.

For the purposes of this story, I chose to send Marie MacLean back to the year fifteen-hundred and ninety, because Angus MacDonald, the eighth Chief of Clan MacDonald of Dunnyveg had been imprisoned by the king due to his feud with the MacLean of Duart, his brother-in-law. The king did in fact induce all those involved in the dispute, being Donald MacDonald of Sleat, Angus MacDonald of Dunnyveg and Lachlan MacLean of Duart, to go to Edinburgh. When they each arrived, they were apprehended and imprisoned. I altered this event slightly, allowing for the MacDonald chiefs' capture by the king's men to suit the story, as I did the ultimate capture of Lachlan MacLean as well.

Sir Lachlan Mor MacLean was the fourteenth Chief of Clan MacLean of Duart.

Angus MacDonald's successor was his son James MacDonald, a minor, and with someone needing to lead the clan, I chose Archie.

Archie MacDonald and Marie MacLean however are fictional characters.

The faerie circle and the amulet, along with its passage down through Mary MacDonald's maternal line were also my addition to the story.

Although the account told by Mary, of Donald MacDonald and his men seeking shelter on the MacLean's portion of Jura, as well as James being taken hostage, Angus's release and his meeting with MacLean at Mullintrea, are as accurate as I could convey them from the historical information on record of this event. Following this tragedy, the feud continued to rage and all within the Western Isles were affected. Ravaging by fire and sword, both MacDonald and MacLean laid waste to huge portions of land.

Lachlan MacLean was killed in action at the age of forty, in the year fifteen-hundred and ninety-eight at the Battle of Traigh Ghruinneart, near Loch Gruinart on the Isle of Islay. He was killed by the forces of Sir James MacDonald, the ninth Chief of Clan MacDonald of Dunnyveg, being Mary and Angus's eldest son who would have been around eighteen at the time.

Lachlan MacLean was buried in the churchyard of Kilchoman on Islay, and he was an accomplished warlike chief who was loved greatly by his clan.

This story is woven with as much accuracy to the period and locations as possible, but any mistakes made are mine alone.

This book forms part of my *Highlander Heat* series, and each within it are stand-alone.

Please feel free to search for any of my other works. I simply adore strong heroines, and have a ton of fun matching them with their honorable alpha heroes.

Also available in paperback
Scottish Historical Romance

Traveling through time…for a Highlander.

Highlander Heat Series

Highlander's Castle, Book One

Highlander's Magic, Book Two

Highlander's Charm, Book Three

Highlander's Guardian, Book Four

Highlander's Faerie, Book Five

Highlander's Champion, Book Six

by Joanne Wadsworth

Looking for more sexy Scottish adventure?

Read on to catch a preview of the next book in the
Highlander Heat series.

Highlander's Charm

Highlander Heat Book Three

by Joanne Wadsworth

Highlander's Charm

Highlander Heat Series, Book Three

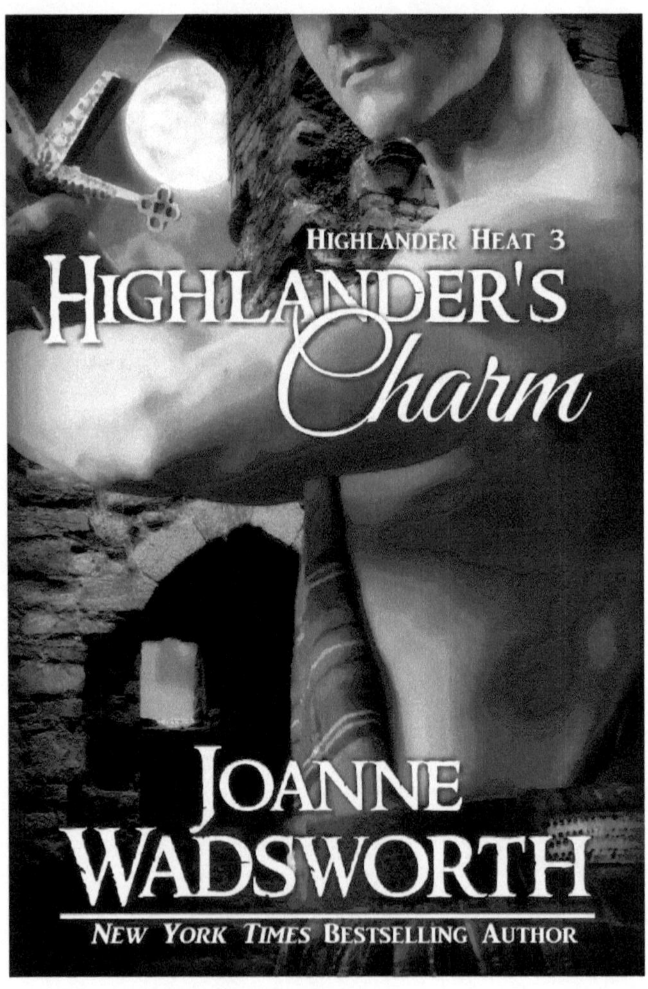

The Fortuneteller

Within the forests of Ardnamurchan, 1569.

Blazing bright, a falling star streaked across the night sky. The earth shook, and deep within the woods, the fortuneteller gripped her walking stick and staggered to her feet. Her campfire sizzled and sparked, and the small creatures of the night scuttled away through the underbrush.

Eyes closed, she reached out with her senses. A portal had opened between times and displaced two souls. Both had been born under a falling star, one mere moments ago, and the other, many years.

Aye, a grandmother and her newborn granddaughter, both with silver eyes giving evidence of their special birth, as it had with hers.

The magic of the stars moved through their blood, only the grandmother had made a pleading wish for the bairn, and it had taken the two of them through time and far from Scotland. They would not return to this place until they once again stood on the land of their birth and made another wish.

Looking deep inside her mind, she searched for aid. A vision shimmered to life. A lad of seven roamed the woods on the neighboring Isle of Mull, his gaze lifted to the sky. Calum too had seen the falling star and sensed the disruption in time, though his eyes held no trace of silver.

Tears streaked the boy's cheeks as he whispered the newborn girl's name. Lila. She was his, and she'd been taken from him, not that he understood how or why.

The fortuneteller shoved her braided gray hair over her shoulder, then from amongst her wrist-full of silver bangles, removed two brass charms. As kin to the grandmother and her grandchild, 'twas her duty to set all that had occurred back to rights. If needed, she would cross time itself to ensure they returned to their homeland.

She handed the charms to her son as he sat across the fire, instructing him to inscribe Calum and Lila's names upon them.

These two pieces would bind them together as their souls already did. Though Lila was special. She would be able to draw on the magic deep within her to make wishes, ones that would come true when she was at her most desperate, as her grandmother had been this eve.

Time itself would not keep Calum and Lila apart.

She'd make certain of it.

The Charms

Duart Castle, on the Isle of Mull, 1590.

"I'll keep us on course toward the sea-gate," Gripping the birlinn's rudder, Calum called to his brother.

Thunder boomed and lightning slashed the rippling waves of Duart Bay with a sizzling crackle, the fieriest welcome home Calum MacLean had ever received. Ahead on the inland rise, the thick stone walls of Duart Castle rose with forbidding height into the night sky.

"Look. Only one of our galleys remains anchored," Colin shouted as he lowered the sail.

"Aye, we'll make haste." Such a sight did not bode well with the depth of the current feud raging between the clans.

Their vessel skimmed the water as it cruised in, and his brother leaped into the waist-deep waves, seized the bow and roped it to a catch alongside the stone mooring.

The call of their arrival boomed from the tower guardsman.

Calum jumped onto the landing and jogged up the trail, Colin close behind him. The portcullis rose from within the stone-arched entrance gate, the clunky sound of its chains reverberating across the moors.

Arthur strode through in his thick fur boots. "Welcome home."

"Where's Lachlan?" Calum's chief had sent him to visit the Chief of MacLeod on Skye and Lachlan should be eager to hear his news.

"On the Isle of Islay. Lachlan received word Angus MacDonald had been captured by the king's men. Our chief didnae care to let this opportunity pass him by. Sixty of our warriors have gone with him. They intend to battle for the Rhinns."

Lachlan was determined to get his land on Islay's western coast back, and with Angus's capture, that would leave the MacDonald clan susceptible without their chief. A prime opportunity indeed, although not one he agreed with. 'Twas time for peace, though it seemed that would never come. "I bring news from my visit with MacLeod. Donald MacDonald too has been captured by the king. Donald and Angus both reside in Edinburgh's dungeons."

"'Tis a boon."

"When did Lachlan leave?"

"A few days past. I expect word soon. Did MacLeod agree to aid us?"

"Nay. With Donald's capture, he insisted there was no need." Lachlan's good fortune had doubled with both MacDonald chiefs in the king's hands. Lachlan would need to keep himself from discovery by the king's men too since they sought all three chiefs in this feud.

The heavens opened and the rain beat down.

"Come, we'll talk further inside." Calum strode into the great hall, Arthur at his side. "Colin and I will gather supplies and sail for Islay."

"That might no' be for the best." Arthur clasped his shoulder. "John MacIan has issued a call-to-arms."

Damn. It seemed every clan surrounding them wished a

fight. It'd been a year since John MacIan's release from Lachlan's dungeons, and if John wished to retaliate, now was the perfect time. As Lachlan's second, Calum would have to remain here in his chief's stead. "Aye, you're right."

"Brother, I can travel to Islay if you wish." Colin shook his dark head, splattering drops over the tapestry covered wall. "I'll ensure Lachlan does no' act too rashly."

"Nay, if MacIan is making his move, 'twould be best for you to travel to Tobermory and join the watchman there. Bring me word of any changes."

Colin wouldn't fail him, as he wouldn't fail Lachlan in his duty to protect their clan.

"Are ye Calum MacLean?" An old woman staggered to her feet from a wooden bench before the blazing hearth. She tapped her walking stick on the floor and jingled the multitude of silver bangles adorning her wrists.

"I am. Who are you?" He crossed and offered her a steadying hand.

"I've been waiting for ye. The past must be set to rights. A woman will come. Ye must keep her safe from the sea, and never let her go."

"What ramblings are these? Again, who are you?"

"Ye are the enemy, yet your heart is pure. She will aid ye, as ye will aid her." She pressed a brass charm into his hand. "Ye were but a lad when she left. I have another charm to gift her, and I shall see it done. Ye are both bound and must embrace your coming visions. Ye will have them because of her, until all things are set right. Allow them to guide ye." She tottered past Colin and Arthur and out the door.

Never had he had a more confusing conversation. The woman should take care she wasn't called out as a witch for her words of foretelling. 'Twas dangerous days for such. "Who is she, Arthur?"

"A fortuneteller, though she didnae admit such. She's been

waiting for your return and wouldnae speak of her concerns with any other."

He faced his brother. "Halt her. She cannae leave in this weather. At least offer her a pallet for the night. Tell her no harm shall come to her if she remains here."

Colin marched out the door.

The charm in his palm heated. *Ye were but a lad when she left.* He traced the inscription lit by the golden glow of the fire's flames.

Lila.
My charm.
Calum.

Lila. Her name resonated inside him. When he'd been just a lad, he'd been hunting in the forest with his father and seen a falling star. Grief had overwhelmed him, so swift and unexplainable.

Needing an answer for what he'd been told, he strode out the door.

Colin stood in the inner courtyard glancing in all directions. "Where is the woman?"

"Gone, Calum. She disappeared with nary a trace."

"'Tis impossible. She must be somewhere." He trotted up the stairs to the battlements and gripped the thick stone crenellation. Beyond, the moors were clear. No fortuneteller.

* * * *

For three nights, he'd been drawn to the eerie silence of the battlements, his soul restless and needy. This eve, the moon shimmered over the still loch, with not the slightest breeze to draw a ripple. The earth shook, and he clutched the charm he'd been unable to release.

Thrice this day the ground had moved so.

Possibly a bad omen. This morn, their warriors had returned

from Islay, though missing their chief and a score of men. Lachlan had been captured and taken to Edinburgh, and their casualties had been great.

Duart was now his to protect from the enemy's hands.

He wouldn't fail his chief, nor his clan.

Pressing the charm to his chest, he closed his eyes.

Solace came when he did.

Chapter 1

On the way to the ruins of Mingary Castle, the seat of the MacIans of Ardnamurchan, Scotland, 2014.

Riding a mountain bike, Lila MacIan negotiated the stony downward trail near Mingary Castle. Birds chirped from the odd pine tree clinging to the craggy hillside, and salty sea spray drifted in the breeze and tickled her nose. This was the way to enjoy nature at its very finest. "How much farther, Zayn?"

"We're close. Mingary's around the tip." Zayn MacKeane skidded his bike to a stop. Gravel thunked the rocks scattered along the grassy verge.

"Thank you for bringing me." She pulled in beside the energetic eighteen-year-old. The sound's blue-green waters glistened under the midday sun. The Isle of Mull, with its grassy moors and forested hills, appeared a lush jewel across the waterway. In times of old, Mull had been the land of her clan's enemy, though that could never take away from the isle's sheer beauty now. If only Nanna was here to see this with her, not missing somewhere in Scotland with the police and her endlessly searching.

"Are you okay?" Zayn nudged her shoulder. "You're

looking lost again."

"I'm fine." Or she would be, once she found her grandmother. "You make a wonderful tour guide. I'm so glad I stumbled across you at the museum and you agreed to bring me." Mingary had been on Nanna's travel itinerary. Where Nanna had intended to go, so would she.

"Stumbled is right." He grinned and rubbed his bruised calf. "You certainly know how to catch a person's attention."

"Sorry." She'd tripped over Zayn as he'd been searching under an exhibit display table with his long legs poking out.

"Since we're kin, you're forgiven." He shot her a mischievous grin.

"Yes, about that. How is it possible we're related? You never said." She'd shown her grandmother's picture to people in his village. So many MacIans, but none had seen Nanna.

"You're a MacIan, and I'm a MacKeane. Same pronunciation, just different letters. That happened a lot in the old days. People mixed up the spelling and it stuck."

"So you're saying we're from the same clan? John MacIan of Mingary's line?"

"Yep, though you have the strangest accent of any MacIan I know."

"In my opinion you're the one with the strange accent."

"So says the Aussie."

"And I'm proud to be one. Oi, oi, oi."

He chuckled. "Why is it Aussies say that?"

"You started it by saying Aussie. It's a chant we like to cheer at sports games, and wherever else takes our fancy. You say Aussie, and I say oi. Now no dissing my heritage or at least the non-Scots side."

"There's nothing to diss on the Scots side. We're a staunch clan and never say a word wrong."

"Now that's a little hard for me to disagree with." Goodness, Nanna would have loved to have met Zayn. He was so funny.

She dug into the pocket of her black Nike sports leggings and pulled out her brass charm. After Nanna had arrived in Scotland a month ago, she'd couriered this coin to her in Sydney. It had provided such comfort to have it close by. Rubbing its smooth disk-like surface, she picked up the trace of letters, an inscription which meant little, yet she adored it all the same.

Lila.
My charm.
Calum.

"That looks old. Can I take a look?" Zayn was the son of the museum's resident historian.

"Be careful with it." She handed it over. "My grandmother received this from a fortuneteller at Edinburgh's markets, or at least that's what she said in her note. It's a MacIan relic from the 1500s. Obviously I'm not the Lila that's mentioned, but it's lovely it holds my name all the same. I didn't even know Lila was Scots in origin."

"I've got a cousin called Lilias. We call her Lila for short. This could be a shortened version too." He smoothed over the etching. "These charms are often referred to as coins or tokens, and this one's in mint condition. You should show my dad. He might know more considering it's inscribed. Did your grandmother tell you anything about it when she gifted it to you?"

"Not much. She said to keep it on me at all times, and to never let it go, which I've done. What do you think about the etching? It sounds kind of romantic to me, like Lila is Calum's charm."

"Hmm, it could be that the piece holds a double meaning. Maybe Calum gifted this charm to Lila?" He handed the coin back. "I'm sorry none of us have seen your grandmother."

"I'm going to find her." She'd never give up her search, no matter where or how long it took her. Tears came to her eyes and she forced them back as she pocketed the precious coin. "Did you remember to bring your wetsuit?"

"Sure did. I've got my snorkeling gear too." He patted his black and blue checked backpack strapped over his shoulders. "Even though it's autumn, I've been known to take a dip right up until Christmas Day. I'm game for a swim if you are."

"When I was wandering about the museum's displays, I read about a storm driving a Spanish Armada ship into the sound. It was a few centuries ago, but it capsized right here at the tip of Ardnamurchan. Apparently a treasure trove of gold coins has never been found."

"I know the story, but I doubt we'll find the bounty. No one ever has."

"I'd love one of those coins." It could finance a broader search for Nanna. The police were doing what they could, but a woman couldn't disappear without a trace. No. She had to do everything she could to find—

The ground shook. Nesting birds cackled and took flight from the trees. They swept down the ridge and along the track in front of her. Feet planted either side of her bike, she waited until the shaking eased. "Does that happen often?"

"We rarely get earthquakes." He thrust his foot into the pedal. "Let's get off this hill."

"Good idea." Loose rocks could easily dislodge and tumble down. She shoved her white shirtsleeves to her elbows.

"Mingary awaits. How about a race?" Grinning, Zayn took off.

"Hey, you cheat. Wait up." Flying downhill, she rode hard in pursuit. Ahead, Mingary's ruins perched on a massive ridge of rock overlooking the sea. The castle's thick walls stood three stories high and exactly as her grandmother had described in her tales. Nanna had spent time here in her younger years and adored this place.

Zayn slowed. "Are you up for a little bit of history on the homeward straight?"

"Absolutely." She'd absorbed what she could at the museum, but Zayn had lived here all his life. He'd be a treasure trove of information.

"John MacIan was the last MacIan to hold Mingary before the Campbell of Argyll took possession."

"I read about that in the archives. MacIan lost his first wife in childbirth, and when he could have wed a woman young enough to bear him children in his later years, he instead married Janet Campbell, his enemy's mother from Mull."

"Yes. Supposedly to bring some calm to the feud that raged through these isles at the time, and usually those kinds of alliances saw success, but in this case it didn't. At the time Lachlan MacLean was the chief across the way, and he was a warrior well known for using any unlawful means to achieve what he wanted. Dad's always talking about that time in history. It's one of his favorite eras."

"I should have brought the book I picked up about the MacIan clan with me. It covered that period. Your father recommended it, but I left it in my hotel room." The wind whipped her hair across her face.

"Watch the dip. It's a bit rough here, Lila."

"Thanks." She lifted off her seat and missed the jarring impact of the bump. "They need to fix this trail."

"The constant rain messes with it, but from here on to Mingary it evens out."

They rode along the final lowland stretch to the bluff.

"We have nothing like this back home. I mean castles and all."

"I've always wanted to visit Australia. Does it feel like you're walking around on your head down there?"

"No." She laughed, something she hadn't done since the

day Nanna had gone missing. "I wish Nanna was here. She'd like you."

"Have you got any other family?"

"It's just me and her." The castle loomed. She pulled to a stop alongside the entrance and propped her bike against the stone wall. The castle's land-gate appeared no more than a darkened doorway leading into its gloomy recesses. "I was expecting a gatehouse and all the trappings. Where is it all?"

"It used to have gate and a drawbridge, but they were lost over time." Zayn butted his bike against hers. "This entrance leads straight into the inner courtyard. Let me show you around."

"Do you come here a lot? It's so close to the village." She crept inside then swept away the cobwebs stretching the width of stone passageway.

"I lived here most of last summer. Dad's on the finance team for Mingary's restoration, and we began the cleanup back then."

"What cleanup?" Moss grew in clumps along sections of the walls. Keeping clear of the muddy rubble littering the path, she jumped from stone to stone. "Sorry, that was rude. You've clearly done a bang-up job. The place looks nice and cozy." She barely hid her grin.

"Funny, but I meant outside. No one's allowed to touch the inside until the experienced crew arrives."

"I see." She rounded the corner, and the sun shone down into Mingary's inner courtyard. The surrounding curtain walls, several feet thick, gave evidence of the castle's initial strength and how it had managed to stand strong for so long. A shame it had been left to go to ruin. "This place must have looked incredible in its heyday. In one museum display, it showed this place had pinkish-white stones."

"They lost their color over time. Plain old gray now."

"Though so much is still intact." She wandered around the open base of a well flooded with water and spilling its excess over the stone floor.

"Careful. Fairly intact, but slippery."

"I'll be—" Her vision hazed, and she grasped the wall. An image materialized in her mind, showing the well's sides rising to waist height with ivy trailing over them. Someone stood next to it in a beautiful olive gown, but as she tried to focus, the image shimmered away.

"Are you okay?"

"Yes, my imagination is playing tricks with me." She was seeing things she shouldn't and it was likely stress. She hadn't exactly been sleeping well since Nanna's disappearance. "Is there anything else I need to watch out for?"

Zayn motioned toward the seaside wall. "There's a small patch there in danger of collapse, but since that tremor we had earlier didn't knock it over, I'm sure we'll be fine."

"It'll be great when this place is returned to its former glory. When will the restoration crew arrive?"

"After the winter." He swung his backpack off. "We should take that swim while the sun is high and leave exploring the castle until later. There's an area outside near the sea-gate entrance where we can change."

"That sounds perfect." She followed him out, collected her gear from the back of her bike then climbed down the steep trail toward the rocky beach. On the loch side, Mingary perched imposingly high on the forty foot rock wall above. Back in the day, the guardsmen patrolling the battlements would have had a bird's eye view across the sound. A prime position.

"Over here, Lila." Zayn waved her toward the rocks.

She sat on a squat stone, lugged her wetsuit, flippers and mask out, then palmed her charm. *Soldier on, my dear. Never give up the fight.* Nanna's voice, words she'd impressed upon her since she was a child, kept her strong. She'd never give up. She'd find Nanna no matter where she was.

"You're holding onto that talisman like a lifeline." Zayn

eased onto the rock next to hers.

"It's the last thing Nanna gave me."

"I'm sorry. I lost one of my grandparents last year. It's not easy."

"She's not dead, just missing." She shoved more of those unwanted tears away and found her inner strength. "I'm sorry you've lost someone close to you."

"Death is so fast. I miss my grandpa. Dad's always got his nose stuck in a museum book, but Grandpa loved the outdoors as I do. At least once a month we fished and tramped together. Those times are long gone now." He stared out over the loch and slowly sighed.

Memories haunted her as well.

"Nanna's always spoken so fondly of this place. She lived here at Ardnamurchan when she was younger and she longed to return one day."

"When did she go missing?"

"A month ago. During her first week in Scotland, she toured Edinburgh Castle, rode the scenic city bus and visited the markets."

"What have the police said?"

"The last person to see her alive was the owner of the bed-and-breakfast where she stayed. The lady told the police Nanna didn't come down in the morning for breakfast, and when she went up to wake her, she was gone. Nanna's belongings still lay around her room, but there was no sign of her. She just disappeared."

"I'm glad you're looking for her."

"I don't know what else to do. I stayed in Edinburgh for a couple of weeks then made my way here. This seemed the next logical place to—" The ground shook again and she clutched the rock underneath her. "That's two earthquakes in such a short time. Do you think it'll be safe to swim?"

"The loch's only a mile or so wide. I doubt a tsunami is

possible. I'm game if you are."

"A swim would be good. Let's find some treasure so I have a ton of money to finance a massive search for my grandmother. The police are doing their thing, but so must I."

"Great. You can change over by the sea-gate wall. It curves around, giving plenty of privacy on the other side." He pulled his white t-shirt over his head and nodded toward the area. "And no peeking at me while you do."

"I promise." She ducked around the corner with her wetsuit, tugged it on and slipped her charm inside her zippered pocket. Her heart ached. She needed her grandmother back. "I miss you Nanna. From the depths of my soul, I wish I could find you, alive and well. I hate that we're apart."

The wind lifted her hair and made it tickle her face. Wishes. What she wouldn't give to have that one answered.

"Are you ready, Lila?"

"Coming." Mask and flippers in hand, she strode toward the shore where Zayn waited on the wet sand. "We're after sparkly and pretty, Zayn."

"Yeah, and plenty of it." He shuffled backward through the surf in his flippers.

She joined him, and at waist depth, popped her tube into her mouth, eased onto her belly and kicked out. Colorful fish darted all around as she swam toward a boulder with its slick rounded top breaking the water's surface. These rocks were everywhere. Hands planted on top, she hauled herself up and sat on the peak. The incoming tide lapped her back.

Zayn tugged his mask down around his neck as he bobbed in the water. "Look behind you. We've got company."

A slick-skinned dolphin grazed the rough stone as the creature rounded it. "Maybe she wants to play."

"There's more than one." Zayn shoved his mask back on and swam toward a second dolphin. "The waters teem with seals too, so keep an eye out. They're not as friendly as the dolphins."

"Thanks for the warning." The dolphin nearest her let out a chorus of squeals then circled the rock she sat on.

"I'm going to try to catch a ride." Zayn grasped his dolphin's fin, and it pulled him out of the water and took off. He let out a loud whoop.

She laughed then stopped as the boulder shook. A wave tumbled her into the water. The current dragged her down and everything blackened.

Fighting to hold onto her breath, she clawed for the surface.

Stars blazed all around, a multitude so bright she slammed her eyes shut. The water sucked her deeper. She had to get out.

An arm clamped around her waist.

She jerked around. A man with piercing golden eyes tightened his hold on her and pointed upward. Yes, upward. That's where she had to go, now.

He pushed them through the murky depths and in a fizz of bubbles, they broke the surface.

She pulled her mask off and gulped in air. "I love you. Where did you come from?"

"Love already, lass? The lights blazed and I dove in." Dark hair was plastered to his face and neck as he treaded water. "Can you swim? The shore is close."

"Yes, but where's Zayn?"

"There's another out here with you?" He searched the water.

"Zayn took a dolphin ride. Hopefully he didn't get caught by the rogue wave like I did. It pulled me under so fast. Goodness, its dark." Afternoon had turned to evening. "How is it so late?" Dizziness overwhelmed her and she grabbed her head.

"I cannae see another. 'Tis only us." His Scots brogue was thicker than Zayn's, his words far harder to understand. Although that could be the head spinning too. She needed rest, or to catch a decent breath.

"He must be okay." He hadn't been near her when the wave

hit. "Please, who do I have to thank for saving my life?"

"Calum MacLean." The waves bumped them together.

"There was an earthquake. I should've taken more care."

"Aye, there've been unusual happenings this day. Thrice the earth moved."

Thrice? Who said thrice anymore?

Behind her, a small island jutted off shore and around it, the waters branched off in three different directions. This wasn't Mingary's beach. "Ah, where am I?"

"Duart Castle on Mull."

Miles from where she should have been. No wonder Zayn wasn't here. "Really?"

"Aye, let's get you to land."

Yes. She'd figure things out once her feet were back on solid ground. She tried to kick, but her limbs shook.

"I've got you, lass." His hold was tight as he cut a fast path through the churning waters, his strength alone propelling them forward. At hip depth, he stood and with his arm around her waist, helped her onto the beach. Frowning, he eyed her. "What is this you're wearing? It looks like sealskin and 'tis equally as dark. I've no' seen such cloth afore."

"It's a wetsuit."

"Has this come from the continents?"

More of his strange speech, and the Western Isles weren't exactly in the backwaters.

"You can buy a wetsuit almost anywhere." She flopped onto her back on the sand. The moon hovered on the horizon, casting a golden wash over the castle's massive stone walls. Duart stood high on the rise of a craggy hill a few hundred feet inland, its fortified walls topped with battlements and tower house windows lit with candlelight. "Zayn will be terribly worried."

"Is he your next of kin?" Calum knelt over her, pressed callused palms against her cheeks. "I'll ensure he's informed you've been found safe and well."

"My grandmother's my next of kin, but Zayn needs to know."

"What village do you hail from?"

"Sydney, though it's hardly a village."

"Are you no' from Mull?" He flattened his palm against her forehead. "Your skin is cold."

"This is my first trip to Scotland, and it appears I took an unexpected detour to your isle at that. And the wetsuit is keeping me warm where it counts." She edged up on her elbows. Along the barbican, guardsmen patrolled the two-story gatehouse. In great plaids no less. She'd read Duart was a fully functioning castle and open to tourists, but this sight was truly amazing. He must be one of the staff. "Do you work here?"

"This is my home."

"You sure keep things realistic for the visitors."

"Lass, your words are odd. I dinnae understand why you speak so." He stared into her eyes. "Aye, and you have the same silver eyes as Mistress Jean who arrived a month past. She too had a strange accent, more like the Lowlanders. What is your name?"

"Lila." She had Nanna's uniquely colored eyes, and he'd said Jean, her grandmother's name. Fingers numb, she clutched his soggy shirtfront. "Tell me what Mistress Jean looks like."

"You're Lila?" Eyebrows soaring, he slid his hands over hers.

"Yes. What does Mistress Jean look like?"

"Elderly. Black hair with a touch of gray. She wore unusual clothing the eve she arrived. What she called pa-ja-mas." He twisted his tongue around the word, as if finding it foreign. "I was in the chief's solar when Lachlan questioned her. She was found wandering this beach, lost and confused."

The hair color was right, and the pajamas were a good sign. Nanna had disappeared during the night after she'd gone to bed, but that had been in Edinburgh, not this far across the country. "What was her last name?"

"Cunningham. After discovering she'd arrived on Mull, she spent some time with the chief's wife. Margaret too was a Cunningham afore she wed and they enjoyed each other's company. She was no' here long, mayhap a sennight afore she continued on."

"To where?" Even though their last name was MacIan, Nanna's maiden name had been Cunningham. It could well be her.

"No' a soul saw her leave. She vanished into the night just as she'd come."

Yes, the timing was perfect, never mind the location. She couldn't let this information slip by without being fully checked over.

"I need to make a call. The person you've described sounds like my grandmother, and she's been missing for the same length of time." Excited, she tugged her flippers off, grabbed his wide shoulders and hauled herself up. Oh, he was hot, hard, and heavily muscled. At his wrist a sheathed dagger glinted, and lower still, his leather pants clung to his powerful thighs. Definitely authentic. She wobbled on shaky legs. "Nice warrior attire."

Frowning, he offered her a hand. "Does your head feel clear? You were under the water for some time."

"My head is—" Her thoughts swirled, and an image flickered through her mind. She grasped hold of the vision.

This man walked beside her across the moors. The late afternoon sunshine bathed his tanned forearms as he opened his hand and stroked a brass coin. "This is mine, so I may keep you close," he said.

"Can I hold it?" she asked him. "Only for a bit."

"Nay, you have your own, and this one I need to keep you close." He glanced ahead at a fallen log barring the trail, scooped her into his arms and carried her over it.

"Calum, you're very good at keeping me close, whether you hold that charm or not." She breathed in the fresh air, picking up an alluring scent. "Where are you taking me?"

"To a place of great beauty." He set her back on her feet at the top of the rise. Spread out in the meadow below, a wash of yellow and red wildflowers swayed in the gentle breeze.

"This is beautiful."

"Aye, though this was a place of great sadness so few years ago."

"What happened to cause that?"

"A great battle. Many of our warriors perished in this field, but now the wildflowers remind all who walk here that our lost kin still live, even though no' among us."

She rubbed her cheek against his shoulder. "You have a soft heart."

"Nay, I am a warrior."

"That too, but your heart's a gooey mess and it's all mine."

"Lila." He growled her name. "You must take care with your strange words. We spoke about this."

"Yes, you spoke and I decided not to listen. Nothing unusual there, and by now, you should be used to it." She grinned, and the sweet fragrance in the air teased more memories to stir. "Nanna used to take me to the markets every Monday morning to buy hoards of fresh stock for the shop she managed. I love flowers, particularly roses."

He kissed the tip of her nose. "As I—"

"Lila?" Calum gripped her arms. "You appear in a daze."

"Sorry, my imagination keeps getting away on me today." Never in her twenty-one years had she experienced a doozy of a vision like that one. She didn't even know this man, yet had recalled a conversation with him as if it were real.

"We must speak." His golden gaze flickered with determination. "I was drawn outside to the loch this eve, as I have the past three nights since I returned from Skye. A fortuneteller told me a woman would come. That I should aid you, and keep you safe from the sea."

"What?" If he truly wished to aid her, all she needed was the use of a phone. She shook the sand from her flippers. "I need to call the authorities. You don't mind telling them about seeing my grandmother, do you?"

"Since my chief's capture, I'm the only authority on this isle. Come." He strode toward the sand dunes, fetched a sword tossed atop a plaid and belted it over his hips. It glinted razor sharp in the moonlight.

"Knowing Nanna might have come through here after her disappearance is the best news. I have to make that call then be on my way."

"'Tis too late to be making calls, and 'tis now my duty to see to your welfare."

"But the police are available twenty-four hours a day." Well, they were in Australia. Surely that was the same in Scotland.

"Again, come. We'll speak inside."

Yes, they would speak.

He'd seen her grandmother and she had to get to the bottom of this.

The way she'd arrived and these visions she'd experienced weren't right.

She needed to sort this. Now.

Highlander Heat

Highlander's Castle, Book One
Highlander's Magic, Book Two
Highlander's Charm, Book Three
Highlander's Guardian, Book Four
Highlander's Faerie, Book Five
Highlander's Champion, Book Six

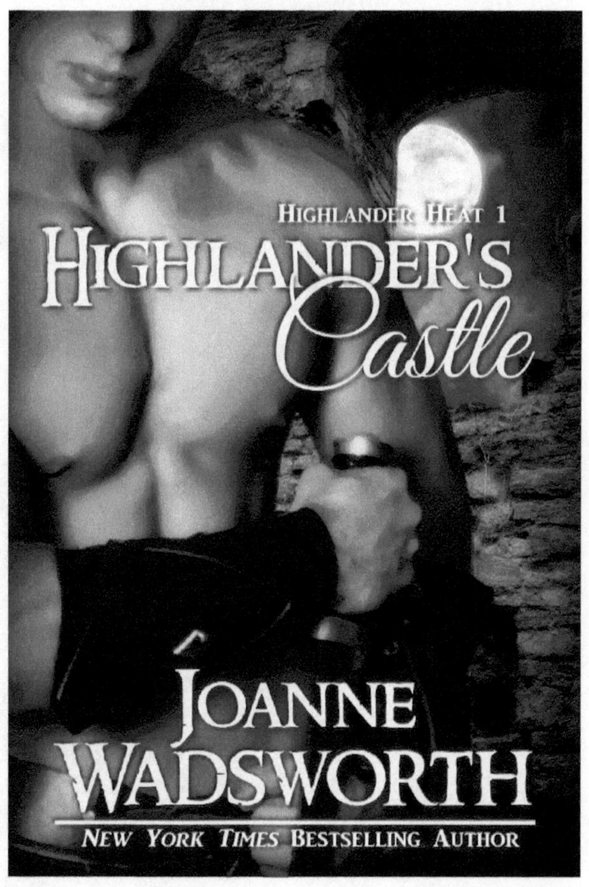

Regency Brides

The Duke's Bride, Book One
The Earl's Bride, Book Two
The Wartime Bride, Book Three
The Earl's Secret Bride, Book Four
The Prince's Bride, Book Five

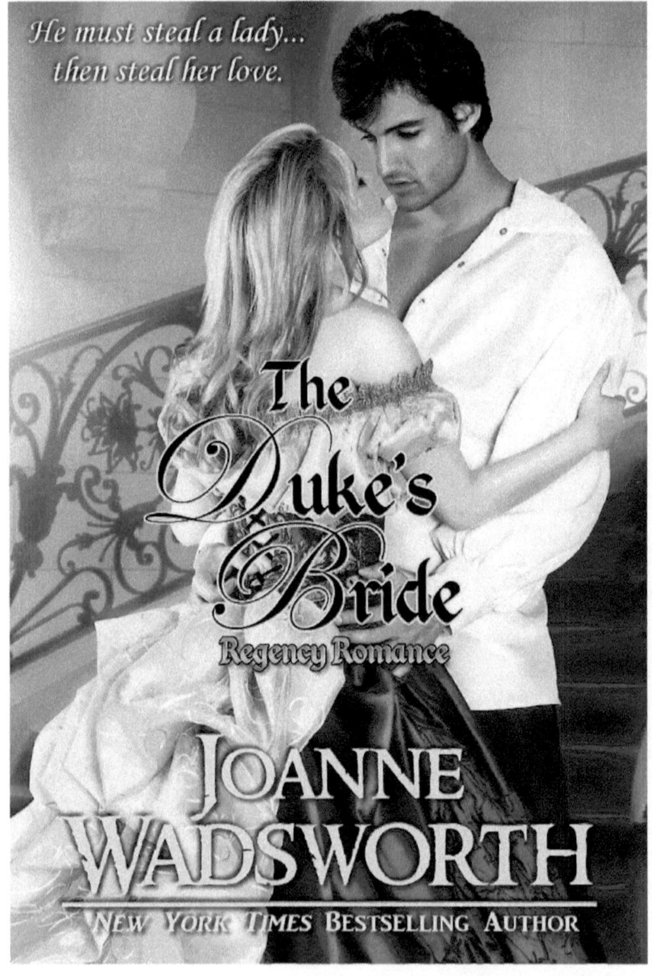

The Matheson Brothers

Highlander's Desire, Book One
Highlander's Passion, Book Two
Highlander's Seduction, Book Three

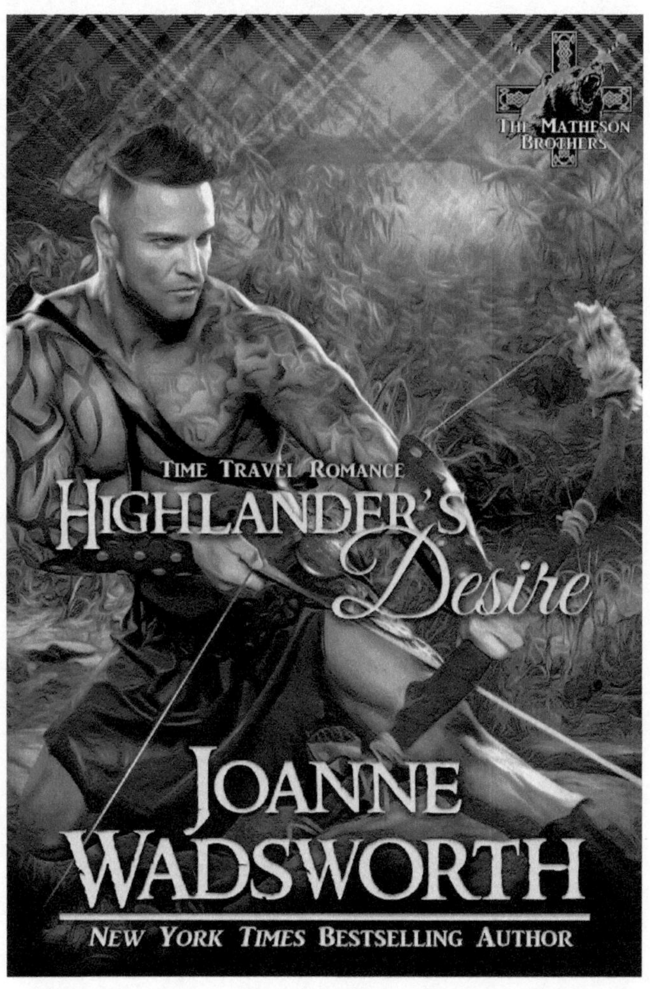

The Matheson Brothers Continued

Highlander's Kiss, Book Four
Highlander's Heart, Book Five
Highlander's Sword, Book Six

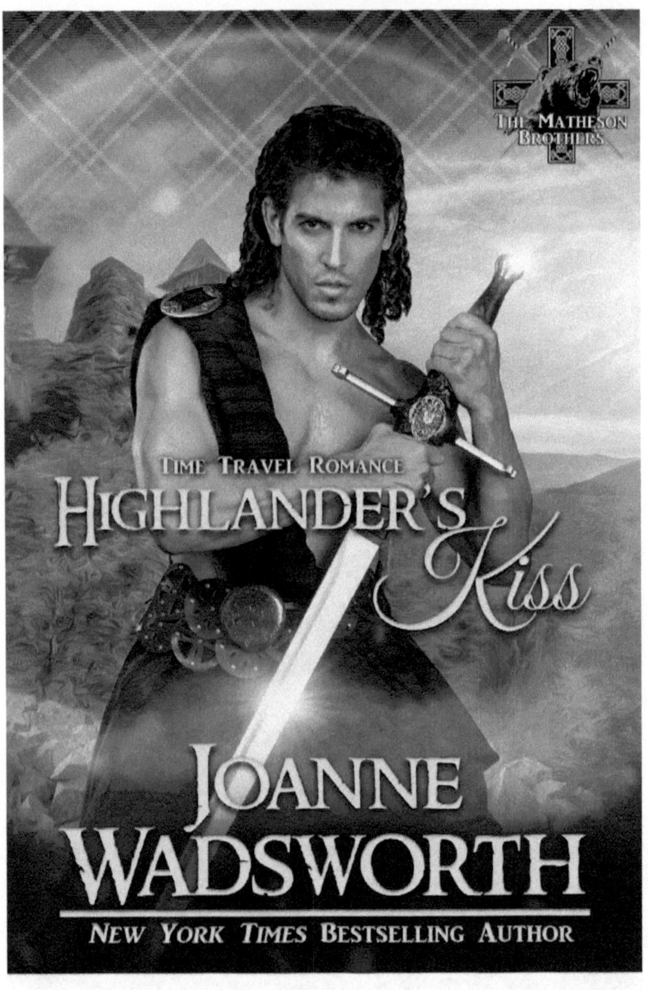

The Matheson Brothers Continued

Highlander's Bride, Book Seven
Highlander's Caress, Book Eight
Highlander's Touch, Book Nine

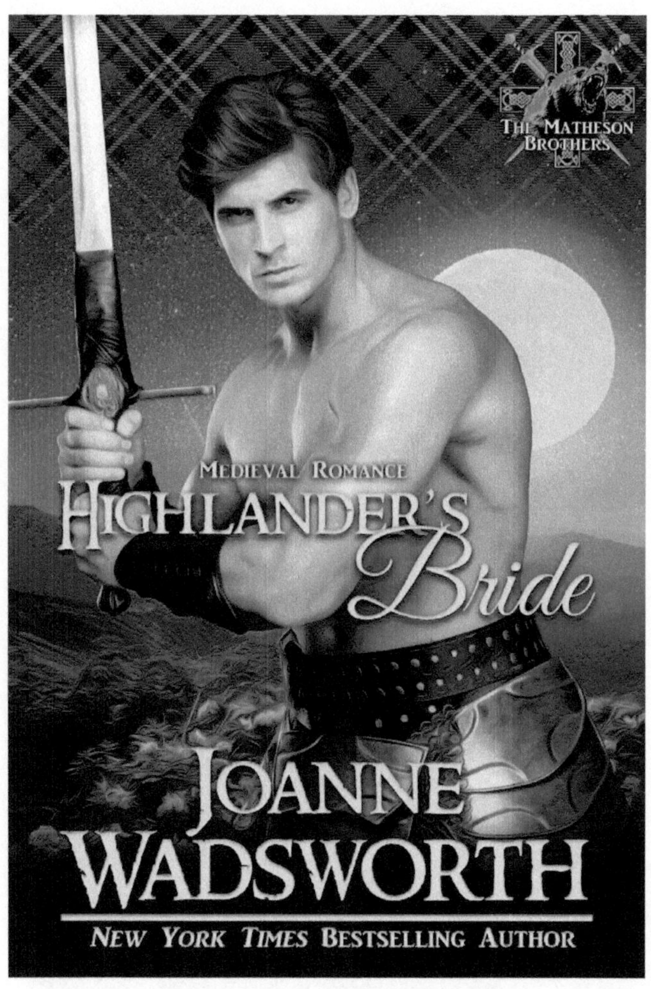

The Matheson Warriors

Highlander's Shifter, Book Ten
Highlander's Claim, Book Eleven
Highlander's Courage, Book Twelve
Highlander's Mermaid, Book Thirteen

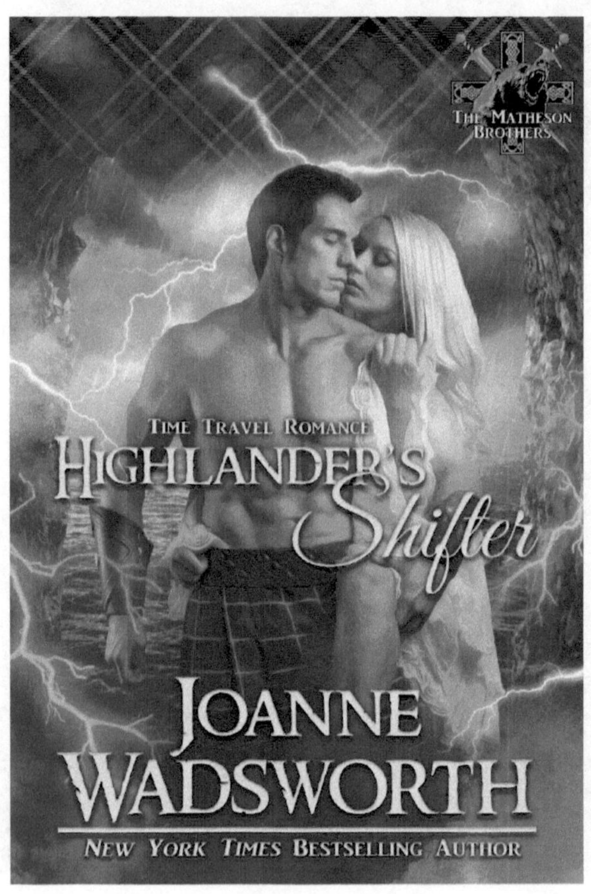

Princesses of Myth

Protector, Book One
Warrior, Book Two
Hunter (Short Story - Included in Warrior, Book Two)
Enchanter, Book Three
Healer, Book Four
Chaser, Book Five
Pirate Princess, Book Six

Billionaire Bodyguards

Billionaire Bodyguard Attraction, Book One
Billionaire Bodyguard Boss, Book Two
Billionaire Bodyguard Fling, Book Three

JOANNE WADSWORTH

Joanne Wadsworth is a *New York Times* and *USA Today* Bestselling Author who adores getting lost in the world of romance, no matter what era in time that might be. Hot alpha Highlanders hound her, demanding their stories are told and she's devoted to ensuring they meet their match, whether that be with a feisty lass from the present or far in the past.

Living on a tiny island at the bottom of the world, she calls New Zealand home. Big-dreamer, hoarder of chocolate, and addicted to juicy watermelons since the age of five, she chases after her four energetic children and has her own hunky hubby on the side.

So come and join in all the fun, because this kiwi girl promises to give you her "Hot-Highlander" oath, to bring you a heart-pounding, sexy adventure from the moment you turn the first page. This is where romance meets fantasy and adventure…

To learn more about Joanne and her works, visit
http://www.joannewadsworth.com